Life Force

David Reynolds-Moreton

sci-fi-cafe.com

sci-fi-cafe.com

Life Force

Chapter 1
The awakening

ZON SAT ON his favourite rock, high up on the mountain top. Or to be more precise, he didn't sit or stand, he just plonked down there, looking out over the sandy alluvial plain beneath, and the rolling verdant hills and valleys which reached out to the distant horizon, where the barren lands began. He often came up here to watch the day end, and observe the meteor display which lit up the sky with its fiery streaks as darkness fell. The green-tinged yellow sun was just about to dip below the horizon, and he always marvelled at the brilliant display of colours which lit up the long streaks of cloud, before the inevitable soft velvet darkness swept over his world.

As the last tiny bit of the sun's crescent dipped out of sight, the first of the brightest stars sparkled into existence - tiny, brilliant diamonds of flickering fire, until the whole sky was peppered with their dancing lights. And then came the meteor shower, tiny bits of space detritus which had been pulled down by the planet's massive gravity to burn up in the atmosphere, leaving thin trails of fiery light in their wake.

Zon always marvelled at this beautiful display, never tiring of its regularity, as there was always something different to see each time. And then he saw something very unusual. One of the meteors didn't have a fiery tail - it was just a shimmering ball of light, sweeping across the sky in a long slow curve to disappear behind one of the hills. It somehow rang a bell in Zon's mind - this had happened before - a long time ago - and the outcome had been far from pleasant.

The alien craft had landed not far from him, so he slid over the intervening ground towards a pile of rocks, assuming a rock-like shape to observe what would happen next. A hatch opened on the craft, and four two legged beings emerged. He thought they had a mean and ugly look about them - even their movements appeared aggressive. Zon wondered how they could remain upright with only two legs, but they seemed to, somehow. The beings wandered about for a while, looking at the different trees, bushes, and rocks, and then they saw a Rockcat, a friendly furry little creature with big brown eyes and a permanent smile on its face. One of the aliens pointed a shiny object at the Rockcat, and a thin beam of light leapt from it - and the Rockcat was no more, disappearing in a cloud of water vapour and little bits of fur.

The aliens made a cackling sound - they seemed to find it amusing. Several other Rockcats came out to see what all the noise was about, and the aliens blew them all to bits as well. Zon could see no reason for this wanton destruction of such friendly creatures, and wondered why they had done it.

Not content with the needless killing of harmless wildlife, the aliens then proceeded to blast several rocks to dust and then a Dingle tree, leaving only the shattered and smoking stump to show where it had been. Zon liked the Dingle trees, as they obligingly swung their branches around to shade him from the heat of the midday sun when he was under them. He would have to stop these horrible creatures from destroying his world - and him too, if they could see him, and realised what he was.

He reached out to them mentally, and recoiled from the hideous stink of the mental image pictures in their minds. These were indeed evil creatures, and there was no place for them in his world. But what to do? There were the sinking sands; if he could lead or guide them towards the sands, that should take care of them - nothing ever came back from there.

Zon slid along behind the four destructive creatures, keeping just out of sight and ready to melt into the background, should any of them turn around. They continued to tramp on down through the valley, blasting anything out of existence which took their fancy, and again Zon wondered why they did this.

Leaving a trail of destruction in their wake, the four aliens eventually reached the edge of a patch of sinking sand. Zon recognised it for what it was because of the extremely fine white particles and the way they shimmered in the starlight. The aliens hesitated at the sands edge, almost as if they sensed the danger.

Before they could turn back, Zon formed a mouthpiece, an air cavity, and throat complete with vocal cords. Filling the air cavity as full as he could, he forced the air up through the throat piece, emitting an almighty roar which echoed back and forth from the surrounding hills.

The aliens looked around in all directions, but all they could see were trees and scrub-like bushes - and a clear patch of sand ahead of them. Not knowing which bush hid the creature with the mighty roar, they rushed out onto the shimmering sands, and slowly sank out of sight, with arms waving frantically. Zon didn't like taking life unnecessarily, and he never did so except in exceptional circumstances. All he wanted to do was protect his world from harm. But that was a long time ago.

Was this bright light in the sky another vehicle full of these destructive aliens, or something else? He felt compelled to find out. Extruding four legs, Zon sped off in the direction he thought the light might have come down in, but it was a long way away and the remaining light level was dropping all the while. Ahead, he could see the outline of one of the highest hills in the area, and he headed for it, climbing its steep slopes in great bounds until he reached the top. By the time he had done so, all the valleys were shrouded in darkness, and there was little hope of finding his target, so he settled down for the dark time, marvelling at the brilliant, coloured stars in the dark velvet of the night sky. He often wondered if they had worlds around them, supporting life in its different forms - but he would probably never know. He was alone, except for the very occasional visitor, and few survived long enough for him to make meaningful contact with.

With the first glimmer of dawn, Zon stirred, but he would have to wait some time for the sun to rise and light up the valleys below before he could continue his quest.

Below him, the hills fell away to the beginning of the desert area of sand and broken rock - and the rising sunlight glinted off something at the deserts edge. The only thing which reflected light was water, and there was no water there. It must the falling star-like thing of the previous night, he thought.

Zon clambered down from his rocky perch on the hilltop, and began the long journey towards the desert area up ahead. It was nearly midday by the time he reached the start of the sandy barren lands, and just up ahead he could see several pieces of shiny metal. The alien craft had come down in a rocky area at the edge of the sands, and torn itself to pieces in doing so, but to one side lay a larger piece of the craft and he headed for that.

This part of the alien craft must have been made of sterner stuff, for it was almost intact - except for a great rent across its middle. Zon approached cautiously, not knowing what dangers might be concealed within the strange shape. Peering in through the rip in the outer casing, he could see a crumpled figure with its limbs contorted in what looked like unusual positions - although he wasn't sure what the usual positions for its limbs should be - they just looked odd somehow.

Extruding a pseudopod, Zon reached into the pilot's compartment and gently lifted one of the limbs. It seemed to still be attached to the creature, but it was a bit floppy to his way of thinking. The creature seemed to be oblivious to his probing, so he reached in a little further, slipping the pseudopod under the main body of the creature and gently eased it out of the piece of equipment it seemed to be encased in. The gap through which he had entered the capsule was too small to lift the body through, so he slowly eased it down again, and extruding another limb, hardened the ends to the consistency of bone. Gripping the two edges of the rent, he slowly pulled them apart, the metal squealing in protest, until the gap was large enough to withdraw the imprisoned creature.

Using both pseudopods, Zon carefully lifted the creature out of the now defunct craft, and laid it down on the ground, arranging the limbs in what he thought was the proper configuration, bearing in mind what his earlier visitors had looked like.

The prone creature seemed to be covered in some sort of fabric, with a transparent covering over its head - from which a red liquid was oozing. Zon decided it had been injured during the impact, and its vital fluids were leaking out. If he was to save its life, he would have to remove the coverings, seek out the actual injuries, and try to repair them. But did he really want to? Was it another evil creature, like the others which had invaded his world?

Zon reached out to the prone figure, trying to pick up any mental image pictures it might have, but there were few which made any sense. The creature was unconscious and totally oblivious to his world, but he didn't sense anything evil about it. Zon felt around the collar of the transparent head piece, found the catches and released them. The headpiece was lifted off, but it took a little longer to discover the fastening of the fabric covering the creature was encased in.

Some while later the creature lay naked on the soft sand, one standing limb bent at an odd angle, and several cuts in its skin allowing a trickle of life fluid to escape. Zon modified the tip of one pseudopod to a small finger like appendage, and ran it along any cuts in the creature's skin he could find, stopping the flow of life fluid and cleaning the wounds with a small amount of sterilizing liquid made for the purpose.

The head wound proved a little more difficult to correct, as the creature was bleeding from one of its hearing appendages - or that's what he thought it was.

Refining the tip of a pseudopod to a fine needle point, Zon slipped the probe into the ear, sealing off the bleeding tubes within, and then flushing away the remaining life fluid which had coagulated on the surface. The bent standing appendage took a little longer to put right. A bone in the appendage had been broken, hence the odd angle at which it lay, so a probe was sent deep into the tissues, sealing off the bleeding tubes and flushing out the now congealing life fluid. Zon realigned the standing appendage to match the other one, and then injected a powerful adhesive into the broken ends of the bone. He though it would hold the ends together long enough for the adhesive to stimulate a knitting of the broken bone. He had used this technique before on other unfortunate creatures of his world, and it had worked for them.

The sun had now reached its zenith, and he knew during the dark time it could get very cold out in the barren lands. Zon thought it best to get his visitor somewhere warmer for the dark time as it was a warm-blooded creature, and as it was in a comatose state its body temperature was too low to lose any heat and survive.

Extruding four appendages from its side, Zon carefully slipped two of them under the still form and lifted it over his back, securing its position with the other two. With one last look around at the defunct space craft to see if anything could be salvaged to aid the visitor's survival, Zon headed off for a known warm place - a deep depression where there were hot springs. It was always warm there, though he had never needed their heat.

Leaving the open plain behind, his four stumpy legs worked rhythmically to speed them both up hill and down long lush valleys, arriving at the warm depression as the sun began to dip towards the horizon. Lowering his burden gently down onto the soft warm sand, Zon wondered what else he could do. The creature's eyes were still shut, and its breathing was shallow and slow. At least it wasn't losing any more life fluid, but would it heal itself? Zon slumped down on the sand - he may as well rest during the dark time, after watching the stars come out. He didn't like to miss that.

In the early hours of the morning, something woke Zon up from a half contemplative rest state. His visitor was in exactly the same position as he had left it, and there didn't seem to be anything else around that he could detect. Perhaps it was the unusual circumstances of the situation he found himself in that had awoken him. Eventually, the sun broke the horizon, flooding the depression in a warm pink light, and Zon moved closer to his visitor to see if there had been any change.

The creature lay flat on its back, just as Zon had left it the night before. The eyes were still shut, and the breathing seemed to be about the same. Perhaps it had been damaged too much for the normal healing processes to cope with. As far as he knew, all creatures he had come across could recover from quite extensive damage, given the right circumstances.

Zon reached out to see if he could pick up any thoughts the creature might be having, but what few there were seemed fragmentary and jumbled up - except for one, which was quite clear. The creature was looking forward to returning to someone, but it wasn't clear who it was, except it seemed to be a hazy representation of another creature like itself. All he could do was stay there and wait to see what would happen, and make sure the creature didn't get too hot when the sun reached its zenith. The two nearby Dingle trees would take care of that though,

Zon went down to the warm water pool, where a thin mist of water vapour curling up from its surface with a life of its own amused him for a moment. He extended a tube-like proboscis to taste the water, as he had never tried warm water before in all his long life. It was, as expected, warm, but it had a delightful, sweet taste to it, so he refilled his water storage sac, and then wondered if his visitor needed water.

Returning to the prone figure on the sand, Zon extruded a thin tube and gently opened the visitor's mouth part. The tube slid in and down its throat, exploring the surface as it went - and then Zon realised that the throat served two purposes - one for breathing air and the other for imbibing food and fluids. He was glad he had checked first, otherwise he might have drowned his visitor. The tube went deeper, and found the stomach, and this was carefully filled with the sweet water.

The green-yellow sun rose and sank several times, but Zon didn't mind as time meant nothing to him. The body still lay prone beside the pool, the eyes shut tight, but Zon noticed the breathing was a little deeper. Perhaps the visitor was recovering a little. And then he got to thinking - if the visitor's eyes opened, what would it see? And would it be afraid? Zon could take on any shape he desired, but what shape should he adopt to not terrify his visitor? He could adopt the form of the visitor itself, but then it would not expect to find any of its kind on this world.

And why had it come here anyway? For the first time in a long while, Zon felt confused and undecided, as he was unable to come to a conclusion regarding what to do about his appearance for when his visitor awoke - if it did.

Once more, Zon reached out mentally to the figure on the sand, and this time the pictures were a little clearer, but fleeting and jumbled up. It belonged to a race who explored space - looking for minerals. Somehow the ship had been hit by some of the meteors which streaked across Zon's sky in the evening, and the controls had been damaged. Zon could feel the terror the creature experienced as it fought to bring the escape module down in a controlled manner, resulting in a very bumpy landing - the ship disintegrating as it careened across the rock-strewn surface. Pictures flashed by of other creatures of its kind - there seemed to be two types. And then Zon understood - some were male and some female - a bit like the animals on his world. But which were which?

And then Zon took a good look at the form before him. Yes, it was the male, having the same feature as the animals he knew. From the random pictures he could see, it seemed that they paired up for life, as far as he could tell. This was different to the creatures on his world, where some stayed together, while others seemed to take partners randomly. The animals on the creature's world were also very different to his. But then he saw no reason why they shouldn't be - these were different worlds.

As the pictures tumbled by, Zon didn't see the aggression and desire for random destruction of his earlier visitors, and this was a relief - as he would not have to contemplate destroying it now - if and when it recovered completely. They seemed to travel around in a variety of strange devices, which didn't seem to have a life of their own. This was something new to Zon; maybe they were like the ship the stranger had come in.

A slight tremble of the ground beneath Zon made him look up - tiny waves rippled across the warm waters, gradually growing in size until they made a soft plopping sound as they broke on the edges of the pool. This had happened several times in the aeons he had been on this world, but they were getting bigger each time, and this worried him, as he could see no reason for it to happen. Slowly the ripples dispersed, and the pool returned to its normal calm surface, with little wisps of water vapour writhing up into the still morning air above.

Realising that he would have to communicate with his visitor at some stage, Zon knew he would have to learn its language - but how? Maybe as it recovered, he could tap into its thoughts, and find meanings for the sounds it used. But so far, these had been few and far between - all he had experienced were pictures and some feelings, along with some odd sounds when its memory looked at incidents containing stress.

A few days later, Zon moved closer to the supine figure, and noticed it hadn't moved since he had laid it out on the warm sands some many days ago. Extending an appendage, he refined the tip to a long needle like shape and slipped it into the flesh where the standing appendage had been broken. The joint had healed perfectly, with a thin band of reinforcing bone around the actual break. Zon was pleased with his work. The breathing rate seemed to be about the same, but now it was much deeper, and the body had a relaxed look about it which he hadn't noticed before - perhaps it was on the way to recovery.

Once more Zon reached out to it - and the pictures were much clearer, along with some emotions. It seemed to be recalling various incidents where it was talking to others, and bit by bit, Zon was able to associate some sounds with their meanings - realising it was going to take some time for him to accumulate enough words to hold a sensible conversation with his visitor.

The days came and went, and Zon persisted in his word learning. Twice he noticed the figure before him had twitched, and then moved the now healed standing appendage. He now had to decide what form to take, should the creature gain full consciousness.

It was two days later, while Zon was watching the meteor shower lighting up the heavens, when he heard a low moan. He moved closer to the figure on the sand, and assuming the shape of a rock, formed a throat, vocal cords and a mouthpiece off to one side so the creature couldn't see it.

'Can you hear me?' asked Zon, surprised at how clear his voice was. The figure gave another groan, and tried to turn its head towards him, but only managed a small amount of movement.

'Where am I?' the creature asked in a faint voice, 'What happened? I can't see.'

'You not worry. I take care of you - help you heal. You must rest to heal, then you will be able to see me.'

The figure on the sand gave another groan, and the head slumped back to its former position.

In all the long time Zon had been on his world, he had never been able to talk with anything - this was something new, and he liked it. The other creatures he had helped to heal after an accident or some other mishap had never used words, although they somehow communicated their appreciation for what he had done. He considered he had the most perfect existence a being could have, at one with all he surveyed - until now. This strange two-legged creature had illustrated that there was another dimension for him to experience.

He realised he needed more words and their meanings to converse easily with his visitor, and over the next few days he reached out many times to its mind for more information. The creature seemed to have led a very complicated life, relying on others for so much, and in turn, contributing to the common good. Relationships with others seemed confusing, with varying degrees of loyalty between them, but to his relief, there seemed to be no overall tendencies towards wanton destruction - unlike the last lot of visitors he had met.

As time passed, the visitor had longer and longer moments of lucidity, and frequently enquired as to Zon's whereabouts, although it still lay prone on the sand. So far, he had managed to evade the queries by changing the subject, but he knew this couldn't go on forever. He would have to show himself in some shape or form sooner or later - but what?

The following day, just after sunrise, Zon saw that his visitor had raised itself up almost to a sitting position - propped up on its elbows.

'Where are you, and what are you?' it called out, and then slumped back down on the sand with a groan. As Zon was behind the creature, he slid to one side next to a pile of large stones, and assumed the shape of a rock.

'Do not be afraid, I am near you, but you can not see me. I have mended your standing appendage and the hole in your head which was losing life fluid. I am doing all I can to make you whole again, please trust me, I mean you no harm. Do you need food or water, and how do I call you?'

'Yes please, my throat is dry, and I am hungry. My name is Bradford, most people call me Brad. What happened, and how did I get here? I don't remember anything after my craft was hit by something.'

'I saw your craft falling out of the sky, and I found you in a piece of it - but you were damaged and asleep. I brought you here where it is warm in the dark time so that you could recover. I will go to the remains of your craft to see if there is any food left there, as I do not know if you can eat food of my world. What does your food look like?' Zon asked, reaching out to pick up the mental image pictures his question called up.

'It's in little square boxes,' Brad replied, 'with the name printed on it.

What do I call you?' He added as an after thought.

'I will go look for your food - I should be back when the sun is high in the sky. Do not worry, I will return to you.'

And with that, Zon slid away from the pile of stones, extruded four legs and hurried off to the crash site.

The remains of the stranger's vehicle lay scattered about on the sandy plain, the main piece in which the visitor had landed laying near the edge of the green area. Zon thought that was the best place to look for the visitor's artefacts – if any had survived.

Holding the mental image picture of the visitor's food packages in his mind, Zon sent an exploratory probe deep into the interior of the vehicle, searching each nook and cranny for the elusive food packages. And then he found them – little blocks just like the picture from the visitor. They were tightly packed in containers, with strange symbols on them – must be different foods for different occasions, Zon mused.

He gathered all the containers he could find, placing them in a neat pile just outside the vehicle, and then continued to probe about inside the craft to see if he could find anything else the visitor might need, but there was little else which made any sense to him. He could always come back, if the visitor showed him any pictures of its needs.

Zon reshaped the top of his body to form a depression into which the packages were stacked, folding the edges over to hold them securely in place for the journey back to the pool.

The sun had reached the highest point in the clear blue sky by the time he had returned to the visitor, who was now sitting up, looking out over the pool of clear water with its back to the approaching Zon, who wondered how he was going to deposit the food packages near enough to the visitor for it to use them without him being seen.

Zon slowed down his approach so that he was almost silent as he moved across the fine sand, and then carefully lowered the containers one by one a couple of meters behind the visitor. Then he retreated into the pile of rocks at the edge of the pool clearing, taking on the shape of a large block of stone. Forming a mouthpiece, he called out to the sitting figure.

'I have brought all the food packages I could find. They are stacked behind you. If you need anything else from your craft, tell me.'

'How did you do that without me hearing you, and why won't you let me see you?'

'I must explain something to you first. I am not like you. You seem to have only one shape, while I can be any shape I want to be, depending on what is needed. I do not want to frighten you because you still need my help to survive here. I will look into your mind to see what shape is acceptable to you – if that is not frightening to you.'

'Yes, I suppose so. Why not let me see you as you are? It can't be all that fearful, surely.'

'I try to explain, I am not of one shape – I can be anything I need to be. If you turn around towards my voice you will see some rocks – I am one of them, or I look like one of them. Are you sure that is acceptable to you?'

The visitor turned its head towards the rocks at the edge of the clearing, shook it several times as if to clear its vision.

'Which one are you?' the visitor asked, and Zon extruded a small pseudopod from the top of his rock shaped body – which just looked like another piece of rock.

'My God, is that you?' exclaimed the visitor, 'You really do look like a piece of rock'.

'I can be any shape or surface finish I need to be, depending on what I want to do'. replied Zon, recalling the visitor did not have this ability.

'What are you exactly,' asked the visitor timidly, 'and are there any more of your kind here?'

'I am the only one – I have never seen another like me in all the time I've been here, and that is a long time. As far as I know, I have always been here. I know of no other place.'

The visitor looked stunned, and Zon wondered if he had said too much, and shown himself before the visitor was ready to observe this new concept of a life form.

'I think you should eat some of your food stuffs, and drink plenty of water so that your body can finish healing itself. The water in the lake is good to drink.'

Brad heaved himself to his feet and nearly fell over. He managed to stagger towards the food containers and picking one up, ripped off the outer packaging.

'I need something to put this in, and then add some water to make it drinkable.' He said, looking around for the missing mixing cup, 'And I need my clothes. I am not used to going around without them.'

'I am sorry, I did not know you needed a container. I think there is one in the remains of your space vehicle. I will get it later. For now, you can use a leaf from the big tree near the lake – just take a large leaf and fold it to make a container. I will collect your wrapping when I get your container.'

Brad staggered clumsily over to the indicated tree, reached up and took down a large leaf, folding it into a cup shape, and then half filled it with water. Dropping in the food concentrate tablet, he waited patiently for it to dissolve and thicken, and then greedily gulped down the soup-like mixture.

'What shall I do when the food concentrates run out?' he asked Zon, looking in the general direction of the rocks, not knowing exactly which one he was addressing as the pseudopod had retracted, having served its purpose.

'I will sample your food and try and find something similar. There is a large selection of fruits, nuts and berries here, so there must be something you can safely eat. The sun is about to go down, and I think you should rest. You might like to see the wonderful colours in the sky, and then the stars – they are very beautiful. You will not need your coverings as it is warm by the lake, and I will see that you come to no harm.'

Brad managed to stay awake until the stars came out, and then drowsiness overcame him, lying dawn near the waters edge to sleep away the dark hours. Early next morning, Zon sped across the hills and valleys to retrieve the drinking vessel and Brad's clothes. When he returned, Brad awoke and saw a strange four-legged creature, a bit like a headless horse with short legs approach, carrying a bundle of cloth.

'So that's what you look like!' Brad said, with a slight tremor in his voice as Zon deposited the bundle on the sand.

'This is the form I use for travelling quickly,' Zon replied 'but I can take any shape I choose, as I have said before.'

'But you don't have a head or eyes, so how can you see where you are going?'

'I don't have what you call a 'head', for travelling. I don't need it, but I do have eyes – they are very small, so you may not have noticed them. Does this make you feel uncomfortable when viewing me? I can make them look bigger if you wish.'

'No, that's alright, it just takes a bit of getting used to, that's all – and thanks for getting my clothes. I don't think I need my space suit right now, that's only if I have to use the shuttle, and that's busted, but I will wear my trousers and jacket. I just don't feel right without them.' He folded the space suit up neatly, placing the helmet on top.

'How come you can change your shape at will?' asked Brad, still not really believing such a thing could happen, 'and what is your real shape - the one you use when you are not changing into something else?'

'I have no real shape, I am just me. I change shape to suit what I have to do - it is more efficient that way. Is there any shape that would make you more comfortable?'

'Yes, if you could look like me - like a human being, I mean. Not exactly like me, but similar.'

There was short pause, and then a humanoid creature stepped out from the cluster of rocks Brad had been addressing. It was the same height and build as him, but dressed slightly differently. Brad gasped and nearly fainted at the sudden sight of another human being when he was expecting... he wasn't quite sure just what he was expecting.

The creature walked right up to him, stopped, and spoke.

'Is this suitable for your comfort? I can change anything you wish, it makes no difference to me.'

'No, that's fine. It's just the shock of seeing another human being - or something that looks like one,' Brad managed to get out between trembling lips, 'this is all so new to me, it will take a bit of getting used to. Thank you for looking after me, I'm sure I'll get used to you, and this world soon. I don't think I'll be rescued, somehow - no one knows I'm here.'

'Why did you come here?' asked Zon, 'Others have come here a long time ago, but they just wanted to destroy everything. They too had a body much like yours, but they looked ugly, and I had to lead them into the sinking sands before they destroyed my world.'

'I didn't intend to come here. My ship broke up around me and I had to use the escape module. This planet was near, and I tried to land here - although I don't remember much about it. If I look like the others, why did you get rid of them and not me?' Brad asked.

'You looked different, and your mind is not full of bad thoughts like them. I did not want to destroy them, but I must, to save my world from harm.'

'I can almost accept that you can change your body shape at will, but I don't understand how you can make clothes like mine out of thin air.' Brad was still grappling with the seemingly impossible, and having a hard time of it.

'What you call clothes is really my skin, I will show you.' And with that the Zon held out his hand, and as Brad watched, the pink skin slowly changed into something looking like the sand they were standing on, and then changed back to skin.

'We must find food for you before you use up your food blocks,' said Zon, 'if you give me one, I will try to find out what it is made of, and then find something here which contains the same things.' And with that he held out a hand.

Brad picked up one of his food concentrates, and placed it in Zon's hand. Slowly the hand turned into a round blob, totally encapsulating the block, and then it turned back into a hand, and the food block had disappeared.

Brad was speechless for a few moments - things were moving too fast for him.

'How the hell do you do that?' he managed to get out at last, 'and where is the food concentrate?'

'I have absorbed it so that I can find out what it is made of,' Zon responded, 'and then I can look for fruit, berries, and nuts that will suit your digestive system.'

'Another thing I don't understand, how come you can speak my language?' asked Brad, still trying to get his head around the fast-changing circumstances.

'When I found you, I thought you were dead. But then you seemed to be in a deep sleep. I can look into your mind, I think that is the word, and I can sense pictures of your thoughts. From that, over many days while you were recovering and mending your broken leg, I was able to build up words which matched your pictures. I may not get every word right, but I am learning each day. Does this disturb you?'

'No, I think you have saved my life - in fact, I'm sure you have. I just don't understand how you can change shape and do other things which seem impossible to me. As for seeing my thoughts, that's what we humans call telepathy, the ability to see others people's mental image pictures. But I don't know if it is real, or just a clever trick some people can do. How do you do it?'

'I have always done this. Not all the time, only when I need to. I just reach out to you and I see what you see.'

'Those trees which bend over to shield us from the sun, do you make them do that?'

'No, they do it because they know we would like that - it is a kindness.'

'Where do you come from? And are there any more like you here?' asked Brad, trying to understand the almost impossible.

'I am alone, and always have been. I do not remember coming here, as you put it. I have always been here. This is my world, and all that it contains must be kept from harmfulness. I am happy to share it with you, as you too are alone. It is very rare for others to come here, but you are welcome.'

'Thank you, and thank you for saving my life. I wish I could understand all that has happened here, but I am trying to. How did you make a body like mine? How did you know what it should look like? It's just like another human being.'

'I looked at pictures you have of your people, when you were recovering from your accident. Now that you are well, what would you like to do?'

'I would like to see some more of your world. It seems to be a beautiful place, from what I've seen of it. Is it like this all over?'

'No, there are seas, desert areas, forests, the Fire Lands, rivers, mountains, and hot areas where nothing grows. There are underground lakes with many creatures living in them, caves that go deep into the world where I have not far in gone - but I would like to, and many other things I think you will enjoy.'

'Why have you not gone into them?' asked Brad, 'surely if it's your world there can't be any place you can't go.'

'There is something I do not understand about the deep cave. I can go in a distance, but then I get the feeling that I should go no further. There is something stopping me, but I do not know what it is.'

'Well, that's one place I would like to see,' said Brad, 'I can't imagine anything stopping you from doing what you want to do.' Zon didn't say anything for a moment.

'I should look for foods that you can eat,' said Zon, 'the foods you have with you should be kept in case we go where nothing grows - and you should go with me so that you recognise the correct plants.' And with that, Zon turned and walked towards the rocks he had hidden in earlier, with Brad closely following.

The rest of the day was spent finding things Brad could eat. Many of the nut bearing bushes provided high protein food, while the fruits selected by Zon proved to be a delight to the taste buds of an ever-eager Brad, the juice dripping down his chin as he sampled flavours he had never experienced before.

The pair had wandered up and down many valleys in their quest for Brad's food stuffs, finally returning to the pool area where he had recovered from the crash.

'You said you did not need your space suit, so why not cut it up to make a carrying device for your foods? That way you can have food with you wherever we go - and some places do not provide food things.'

'I don't have the tools to cut it up and sew it together into a bag,' said Brad, 'and if I did, I don't have any thread, and the material is far too tough to tear by hand.'

'I can help you,' offered Zon, 'just show me where you want it cut, and I will do it.'

Brad laid the space suit out on the ground, a puzzled look on his face, and showed where he wanted the panels cut. Before his astonished eyes, Zon extended a finger which flattened out and developed a sharp edge, glistening in the sun, much like a ceramic knife. Within minutes, he had sliced the suit into the sections indicated by Brad, and the finger returned to its normal state.

'What do you need to hold it all together?' asked Zon.

'I'll need a needle and thread,' Brad replied, and I'll bet you can't produce that!'

'I do not think I can do that,' Zon responded, 'but I can stick two pieces together if you lap one edge over the other.'

Brad picked up two pieces of the space suit, lined up the edges, and Zon extended his finger again which grew a small tube-like section. He then ran it along the seam - a thin line of some clear liquid seeped out, and the edges of the two pieces of fabric became as one.

'My God!' exclaimed Brad, 'that's neat!'

'It is the same principle I used to mend your broken leg.' Zon said, as though it was something he did every day.

Very soon they had made a substantial carry bag, complete with shoulder strap and covering flap.

'You say you would like to see my world - the hot lands are not far away, and just beyond them are the Fire Lands.'

'Surely they are one and the same thing.' said Brad.

'No, there is a difference, as you will see.' Zon replied, 'From the pictures I picked up when you were lying still, you know about mountains that bring forth liquid rock and fire - the hot lands are not like that.'

'OK, let's go there - it sounds interesting. But we'd better load up with food stuffs first. By the way, what do you eat?'

'I eat, as you put it, very little - just enough to make up for anything I make - like the glue stuff I used to make your carry bag. Do you wish to walk on your legs, or would you like me to change my shape and carry you?' asked Zon.

'I think I would like to walk,' replied Brad, not comfortable with the shape changing habits of Zon, 'Now I've got my legs back, I'd like to use them.'

They set off at a good pace, leaving the pool and shade trees behind them, and out into the open valley which stretched out almost to the horizon. It wasn't long before Brad slowed up, his legs aching from the unaccustomed usage, and asked to take a break.

'Don't you ever get tired?' asked a somewhat embarrassed Brad, sitting down on a convenient rock.

'No,' replied Zon, 'I am made differently to you. Your legs will get better as you walk more, or so I would think. You did have a lot of damage when I brought you to the pool, that is why I offered to carry you.' Brad now wished he had accepted the offer.

After several more stops, the terrain changed. Gone was lush green vegetation, colourful bushes and trees, the ground became stony with patches of fine orange coloured sand, stunted bushes struggled to survive in the barren dry surroundings, and then they came across the first of the fumaroles. A little mound some thirty centimetres high, with a small hole at its top, was emitting a stream of what looked like smoke. Brad bent down to sniff the grey haze and wished he hadn't.

'My God, that smells foul,' he exclaimed, 'something has died down there, and rotted, or is it just vaporised minerals?'

'I do not know,' replied Zon, 'it has always been like that. All the little mounds smell like that - the big ones are worse, and they have a yellowish smoke,' he added.

Several other fumaroles were looked at by Brad, and then they came to a big one, issuing a pale yellow smoke.

'My God, that stinks something awful,' said Brad, backing off, 'I think I know what's making the smell. We call it sulphur - there should be a yellow deposit around the inner edges if I'm right,' he leaned forward, holding his breath, 'yes, there it is, a very useful material,' and he broke off a small piece and held it out to Zon.

'What can I use it for?' asked Zon, a puzzled look on his face.

'I didn't mean for you to use it,' Brad responded, 'we use it as a chemical to make other things.' Zon nodded his head, as he now thought he understood Brad's meaning.

Further on they came to a split in the ground, a rift some ten metres long and about four metres deep. At the bottom of the rift, a thick black liquid bubbled and seethed, and a strong smell of hot tar pervaded the air.

'You've got oil here,' exclaimed Brad, 'a natural spring of it. We have that where I come from, but we usually have to drill deep down in the earth for it. There must have been a sea here at one time, and it got covered over with a deep layer of rock; the sediment at the bottom must have contained animal life, and the heat and pressure turned it into oil. Do you remember a sea here?' he asked Zon.

'There are many seas on this world, some large, some small. I think you refer to them as lakes. I don't remember a sea here, but it is a very big world, and although I have been here a very long time, I have not seen all of it.'

Brad could feel the heat from the ground as they walked along, and it was getting hotter. Soon, jagged lumps of rock protruded from the surface, dark and menacing, and Brad slowed his pace.

'Do you feel it too?' asked Zon, 'That is what I feel when I am in the deep caves.'

'You should be able to override it,' said Brad, 'I can - just push ahead, but be careful not to touch them. That is the feeling I get.'

As they progressed, the dark rocks became more numerous, and they had to thread their way carefully through them. Then Brad noticed the multi-coloured crystals embedded in their surface.

'There's a fortune here,' he exclaimed, 'these look like what we call 'precious stones'; diamonds, rubies, sapphires, and God knows what else. If I could get them back to my home world, I would be very rich indeed.'

'They are just coloured stones,' said Zon, 'so why are they worth so much?'

'That's just something my people think valuable - mainly because they are rare, and hard to get, and when they are cut and mounted, are very beautiful. People wear them - mainly, I think, to show how wealthy they are.'

'So, if a thing is rare, your people consider it valuable? I do not really understand that.' Zon replied.

'Put like that, neither do I,' Brad replied, with a laugh, 'it seems one has to be in a situation like I'm in to understand real values. I mean, food is more valuable to me than those stones.'

As they left the rock-strewn area, Brad's hand brushed against a rock, and he felt a sharp tingle, like an electric shock. Something was warning him not to touch the rocks - or their multi-coloured gems.

They were back on sandy ground again, with the odd withered bush doing its best to suck enough moisture from the dry surroundings to survive, and having a hard time of it; and then they were back in familiar territory - green grass underfoot, bushes and small trees, most of which bore fruit or berries of some kind. They both sat down on a grassy mound, and two Dingle trees obligingly swung their branches over them to shield out the heat of the sun.

'So where now?' asked Brad.

'I suggest you eat something; you need to replace the energy you have used,' said Zon, 'and then we can continue on to the Fire Lands. But they are very hot, and you may not be able to tolerate that much heat.'

Brad nodded, and delved into his carry bag, 'Do you want something?' he asked.

'No, I don't need anything, thank you,' Zon replied, with a smile, 'I do not use energy like you do; but I think you may need water soon, so we will look for some.'

Chapter 2
Into the heat

AFTER THEY HAD rested a while, Zon got to his feet and beckoned Brad to follow him, the Dingle trees lifted their branches back to their normal position.

As the sun began to dip towards the horizon, they came across a crystal-clear pool of water surrounded by trees, and Brad drank his fill.

'It would be wise to stay here for the night,' Zon said, 'the sand around the pool will retain some heat from the sun, as you are heat sensitive.'

'What do you mean?' asked Brad, 'don't you need warmth?'

'No, not in the sense you do,' Zon replied, 'my body stays the same temperature, no matter where I am. I do not know how it does that, but it always seems the same.'

As the sun slipped below the horizon and the stars came out, Brad tucked into his food bag, not realising just how hungry he was.

'That's odd,' Brad said between mouthfuls, 'the sun's gone down and the sky is nearly black, but we have light here. Where's it coming from?'

'If you look up into the trees, you will see small pinpoints of light. They are what I call Light Flies - I think you call them beetles. They have an interesting life cycle; the flies give out either a pale blue light or white light. A blue fly will mate with a white one, and then the white one goes down to the water the wings fall off, and the fly swims down to the bottom of the pool. Once there, it seeks out a worm which lives there, and lays its eggs in the worm. The eggs hatch into tiny grubs which live off the worm. When the worm dies, the grubs are released and float to the surface where they crawl out and wait for a small passing animal, they then attach themselves to the fur of the animal, and live off the dead skin cells the animal sheds - so the animal is not harmed. When they are big enough, they grow wings and fly up into the trees - and the whole cycle begins again. It took me quite a long time to find that out.'

'Sounds a bit like my world,' said Brad, 'everything lives off something else, from the smallest creature to the largest animal - and we humans are no different!'

'Look up to the sky,' Zon said, 'see those bright lights racing across?

That is how I found you. One light looked different, it did not burn out like those do, so I went to see what it was - and found you and your crashed ship.'

'I'm glad you did,' Brad replied, 'if you hadn't, I wouldn't be here now - enjoying your world.' He thought Zon smiled in the pale glow surrounding the pool, but couldn't be sure it wasn't just a trick of the light.

'You sleep now,' said Zon, 'I will wake you when it is light again.'

Brad suddenly felt very sleepy, and wriggling down into the soft warm sand, his eyes closed, and he slept a dreamless sleep.

The sun came up, and the stars faded for another day. A quick dip into the food bag and a drink for Brad, and they were ready for the next stage of their journey of exploration.

Leaving the pool area, the ground soon lost its cover of green, and rough stones dotted the sandy trail. Ahead, a high cliff reared up into the skyline, dark and menacing. Meanwhile, Zon had gathered up some dried sticks, and Brad wondered why he had done so, but didn't like to ask.

'We shall have to climb that,' said Zon, 'I have only been up there once, a long time ago, but there is a way up.'

Brad took one look at it and gulped. It looked sheer, but he took Zon's word for it that it was climbable. As they approached the cliff face, a slanting ledge, a metre or so wide, rose and disappeared into a hole. All trace of anything growing had long since disappeared, and the ledge seemed to be covered in a fine dust. In places the edge had broken away, and it was only just wide enough for them to walk along. The ledge snaked around buttresses of rock which stuck out to impede their progress. As they approached the black hole in rock, Brad felt nervous for the first time.

'It's as black as pitch in there,' Brad exclaimed in a faltering in voice, 'how can we see where we are going?'

'I have some sticks, which we will light.' replied Zon, picking up and discarding several stones. At last, Zon the found the one he was looking for, a hard looking flint-like nodule. Extending a finger, which turned into what Brad thought of as a blade, Zon proceeded to scrape one of the sticks, producing a small pile of shavings along with some wood dust.

Zon struck the flint on another piece of rock, and a small shower of sparks landed on the dusty pile of shavings. A couple of puffs, and the shaving caught light, and then the bundle of sticks.

'How did you know how to do that?' asked Brad, impressed.

'What you call a logical thought process. We need light, sticks burn and produce light. Some hard stones, when struck with another, produce sparks. Plant dust and shavings will catch fire easily - we have the light we need.' Zon replied, as though he did it every day.

With Zon in the lead, they entered the black hole, their footsteps making a strange echoing shuffling sound. The dark surrounding rocks seemed to suck the light from the torch, leaving just enough to see their way.

'Be careful,' Zon called out, 'there is a hole in the path just ahead, you will have to jump over it.'

Brad looked at the gaping drop at his feet in the flickering torch light and knew he couldn't.

'There is no way I can jump that,' he exclaimed, 'it's nearly three metres across.'

'Yes, you can,' replied Zon, 'I will help you. You hold the torch while I go across.'

Zon took four quick steps and leapt into the air, nearly knocking the torch from Brad's hand. He seemed to sail across the yawning gap, to land safely on the other side.

'Now you must jump,' Zon said, 'I will extend my arm, you hold onto it. You must jump high, and I will pull you across, but first throw the torch across. No, I will reach for it.'

Brad was suddenly soaked in a sweat of fear at the thought of it, as Zon's arm turned into a long thin rope-like appendage and extended across the gap. Taking hold of the torch, it left Brad's trembling hand and was then held aloft to light the hole beneath his feet. Before he could do anything, the rope-like arm of Zon had shot out to curl around his arm, and he felt a slight tug.

'You must jump high.' Zon called out, a shadowy figure on the other side of the hole.

Brad took a few steps back, Zon's arm extending to keep contact; and with his heart in his mouth, he sprinted for the black hole in the tunnel floor. As he rose in the air, he felt Zon's arm extension shrink, pulling him across the blackness below, to land in heap on the other side.

'I didn't like that much,' said Brad, gasping for breath, 'I really thought I was a goner.'

'You were quite safe, I would not have let you fall.' said Zon, pulling Brad to his feet, 'We had better hurry, the torch will not last much longer.'

Together they tramped on up the sloping tunnel in the rock, the torch getting shorter by the minute, and then they were out in the open. It was bleak, dark grey, with the odd outcrop of black rock, and windswept. Deep valleys lay at the base of towering sombre looking piles of rock which reached up into the sky, and a metallic smelling dust floated in the air. Together, they picked their way ever upwards until they came to a flat ledge, which overhung a deep valley. At the valley bottom could be seen a river of lava, the turgid mass slowly creeping along, and making a faint crackling sound.

'Where does that lot come from?' asked Brad, peering over the edge of the precipice.

'A long way away,' Zon answered, 'it pours out of the top of a very high hill, I think you call it a mountain, and runs down the valleys. I do not know where it goes after that, I have not looked.'

'How far up here have you come before?' asked Brad.

'Only as far as this. I did not see anything interesting here, so I went back down to the green valleys below. It is more pleasant there.'

Just then, Brad noticed something and pointed at a block of stone.

'That's not natural,' he said, 'that's been cut into a neat block. Someone else has been here, unless you did it.'

'It is not my work,' Zon replied, 'I do not cut stone. But you are right, something has. Let us explore, we may find some more.'

Further along the ledge they were in for the next shock. A set of steps had been carved into the living rock, leading ever upwards, and disappearing into the haze above.

'Do we go up there?' asked Brad, 'it might lead to something which will give us a clue as to who made these steps.'

'I think we should,' replied Zon, 'but we must be careful not to be seen if here are others up there. I have never seen anyone else like us, except for those who come here from the sky, and I don't think they did this.'

The pair began the long climb up the stone stairs, Brad saying that no one had used them for a long time as they were covered in fine dust, and there were no footprints.

About halfway up, they came to the remains of several walls, built of cut stone, but only the lower portions remained, the rest possibly having fallen over the edge to the valley below.

'Look,' said Brad, 'that small tower on the end of the ledge, it looks like what we would call a bell tower - there's no bell, but there's a bar it could have hung from.' Zon just nodded, but said nothing.

They went over to the tower, and began to climb a set of stone steps let into the outside wall, but had to give up, as the steps spiralled around the tower, and several higher up were missing. Down on the flat area again, they approached the next flight of steps leading to the plateau above, and although covered in dust, they seemed to be older, going by the wear marks.

As they approached the flat area at the top of the steps, Zon, in the lead, called out.

'This will interest you; as you say, someone has been here before.'

A flat half moon shaped area of smooth rock lay before them, with the mountain rising behind it. Set back up against the rising rock face, stood a stone building with high set windows and a large inviting door. What looked like a tall bell tower rose from the back of the construction, complete with conical roof.

'I don't believe this,' exclaimed Brad, 'this is too much.'

'Why do you not believe what you see? It is there.' Zon said, not understanding the nuance of what Brad had said.

They approached the solid-looking building cautiously, not knowing if any inhabitants would come rushing out to challenge them. But the place looked abandoned.

'This place reminds me of what we had in ancient times,' said Brad in a hushed voice, 'it's called a monastery, where people of a religious nature used to live and pray.'

'I do not understand the word pray.' Zon replied, 'Could you look at it in your mind, and what religious people are, and do?'

Brad did so, and Zon nodded his head in acknowledgement.

'I do not understand why people do this. Who do they pray to, and for what purpose?'

'It's something people did a long ago, I never saw any sense in it.' Brad replied, and the subject was dropped, as Zon thought it of little importance.

The door looked very solid, but they couldn't make out what it was made of. A lever to one side of the door seemed to be the method of opening it, and Brad tried to move it, but it remained firmly set in place.

'There is a small knob just there,' said Zon, pointing to it, 'it must have a purpose.'

'Looks like some sort of decoration to me,' Brad replied, 'I'll give it a push.'

Brad pushed the knob, and it sank back into its recess, followed by a faint click and the lever dropped a fraction. He pushed the lever down; the door emitted a creak and opened a few centimetres. Zon gave it a push, and they were in the old building.

Several stone benches were set against the walls, and in the middle of the room was a raised area with a solid looking set of railing around it. Brad went over to it and stepped onto the plinth to peer over.

'Hey, come and look at this,' he called out, 'there's a hole here going down to one hell of a depth, and something is glowing at the bottom.' Zon joined him and looked over the railings.

'That is molten rock,' he said, 'just like what we saw in the valley, but it is a long way down. This part of the barrier looks as if it is moveable.' He added, lifting a small lever, and a section of the railing swung open. And then they saw above their heads in the gloom, a metal cage suspended on a chain, and a winding mechanism next to it.

'That smacks of something rather nasty,' said Brad, 'I don't think they used it for cooking, at least not food.' Zon just gave one of his nods.

They left the plinth and walked to the other end of the room; as they approached the end wall, a section of the floor gave a little, and a door opened in front of them.

Ahead was a small flight of steps, and then a corridor with ledges along each side adorned with some of the most grotesque heads Brad had ever seen.

'My God, they're ugly,' he exclaimed, suppressing a shudder, 'they look humanoid, do you think they're real?'

Zon went up to one of the heads and poked it with a finger - Brad thought it was a finger, but it had a tiny silver coloured probe on its end.

'Yes, it would seem they are life size, and have been preserved in some way. As you say, they are ugly, much like those beings who wanted to destroy my world long ago.'

At the end of the short passage, they came to a junction, one leading to the left, and one to the right. Undecided, Brad leaned against the wall trying work out which way to go, when a section gave way behind him, rotating to reveal another passage behind. Brad stuck his head into the opening, and in the dim light could just make out a tiny pinpoint of light on the opposite wall a few metres away. As he eased himself into the opening, he noticed what looked like a locking mechanism on the edge of the moving slab of wall and drew Zon's attention to it.

'It looks like a device to hold the wall in its shut position,' said Zon, 'but it has been broken. I would think a heavy blow has been used by the way it is bent.'

'I'm going in,' said Brad, 'I want to see where that light is coming from.' He stepped into the hidden passage and went along towards the light on the back wall. 'It's very narrow in here,' he said, 'and a bit musty, but I can....hey, you must come and see this,' he exclaimed, 'the light is coming from a small glass-like bead set in the wall, and if I put my eye to it, I can see into the passage where you are.'

Zon joined him, and thought it was spying device for those in the hidden passage. They moved along several metres until they came to another splash of light on the back wall, and putting an eye to it in turn, they were looking into another room.

'It looks like an operating room, with all those instruments on that table,' said Brad, 'but there is no clue as to what they were operating on - surely not themselves.'

They moved along to the next splash of light, some five metres away, and were in for another shock. This room contained several metal cages, and in one of them, a humanoid skeleton lay distorted and crumpled up. Several other spy holes revealed many more rooms, some very small, others of more normal size, but all empty.

'Let's go back the other way,' said Brad, 'this is a terrible place, but I would like to know just what they were up to here.'

They squeezed their way back to the entry point, out into the main passage and down the next section. One room was obviously a place where they had their meals - long tables and benches, with a few bowls and crude plates lay scattered about, and a dimly seen hatch through which the food could have been served. Next to the eating room was a store - large pots arranged on shelves no doubt held the ingredients for their meals, and on the floor were a pile of bones, much larger than human remains. And then there were a series of sleeping rooms; crude beds made of what looked like wood, although it was very dark in colour and looked more like stone. A rough table and chair completed the occupant's merger belongings.

The next room looked as if it had been where they wrote, small desks complete with chairs lined one side of the room, while the other side was taken up with shelves stuffed with what might have been the books they wrote - it was difficult to be certain, as most had decayed in to piles of dust.

Along the way, several other narrow passages led off to other sections of the building, but there were too many to be explored before the daylight failed. Somehow, one of the secret doors had been left open a little, and the pair squeezed in to see where it would lead. They came to a spiral stone staircase eventually, and Zon thought it might lead to the tower they had seen from the outside of the building.

'Where is the light coming from in here?' asked Brad, 'There have been no spy holes for some time, but we can see reasonably well.'

'It's almost as if the walls themselves give out a little light,' Zon replied, 'although I do not understand how that happens.'

Several spots of light appeared on the wall as they reached the top of the tower, and peering through the spy holes, the bell tower room was seen. A massive bell hung from a frame set in the ceiling, and next to it was a metal chair fixed to the floor, with arm rests, and securing chains dangled down waiting for an occupant.

'Any poor sod strapped in that chair would have had his eardrums blasted out', exclaimed Brad, 'and it would have been very painful. Look, there's a lever down here, maybe the spying people could operate it from here.' And with that, Brad pushed the lever downwards.

A blast of sound rang out as the sonorous tone of the giant bell reverberated through the tower, both of them clapping their hands over their respective ears.

'That must have caused much pain for anyone in the chair,' Zon said, as the boom of the bell faded away, 'why would anyone want to do that?'

'Maybe they were like those people who visited you long ago, they seemed irrational and cruel from what you've said. What do you make of this set up?' asked Brad, not finding a rational explanation for what they had seen.

'It would seem there were two lots of people here,' Zon replied, 'those who lived in the main part of the building, and those who spied on them. Maybe those who spied made the others do cruel things, or maybe they were just cruel, and the 'spiers' liked to watch. None of it makes much sense to me, but I am not what you call humanoid. Let us see if there is a way into the bell room. Night is soon coming, and you cannot sleep well in this confined space.'

When pushed, a small stud sticking out of the stonework rotated a slab of wall, and they were into the bell room.

Brad lay down on the floor after a small meal, he didn't feel like eating much after all the unpleasant things they had seen, but knew he must keep his energy levels up.

As the sun shone through the window holes in the bell tower next morning, Brad awoke from his slumbers to find Zon at one of the holes, looking out into the distance.

'What are you looking for?' asked Brad.

'I can just see the top of a mountain I recognize, but from a different angle. I think it is the same one though. I think we should go there, if you have seen all you want to here.'

'Yes, that suits me fine. I've had enough of this sad place; it was interesting, but I prefer your green valleys.'

'We shall have to go down to ground level. I suggest going down the tower rather than those tight passages, and then find a way out of this land of fire. There should be another way out, rather than returning the way we came. You should eat first.'

There didn't seem to be a normal door out of the tower room, and then Zon found a trapdoor in the floor, and they were on their way down a much wider set of steps.

Part way down they came across a door set in the wall, and being inquisitive, Brad suggested they explore. At first there didn't seen to be any way of opening it, and then among all the other ornamentation, Zon found a pattern of studs in the middle of it, and they moved. They both tried pushing each stud in turn, but nothing happened.

'It must be a kind of lock, so when the studs are in the correct place, something should move - and that will make a sound.' Zon said, with the kind of certainty Brad was slowly getting used to.

'I didn't hear anything,' said Brad, 'and I've got good hearing.'

'It maybe a very little sound, otherwise others would be able to work out the combination,' Zon replied, 'I am sure your hearing is very good, but I think we need something different here.'

Much to Brads horror, (without thinking, he was getting used to looking upon Zon as a normal human by now) a thin tube exuded from behind Zon's ear until it touched the area near the lock system.

'Press the studs in one at a time, and then release them. I will tell you when you have the correct ones.'

Brad did as he was bid; some minutes later, there was final click, which even Brad heard, and the door swung open. The room was small and circular, hewn out of the living rock. Zon thought this part of the tower was up against the mountain, as there was no sign of stone blockwork. Hanging on pegs were four full length thick leather coats, with fleece on the inside.

'Looks like somebody expects cold weather,' exclaimed Brad, 'I don't see why they would need them up here with all this heat.'

'Perhaps they have to travel into a cold region for some purpose,' responded Zon, 'but the nearest cold region is a long way away, so maybe there is another reason for such heavy clothing.'

Brad reached up to feel one of the coats, and where he touched it, it crumbled into dust,

'It must have rotted, but that would take ages.'

'I think this place has not seen anyone here for a very long time,' said Zon, 'it is strange that I have not seen any sign of these people in my travels, and I travel a lot.'

Opposite the door they had come in by were a series of faint lines in the rock face, and Zon went over to it.

'This looks as though a hole has been blocked up, or maybe it is a hidden door.' said Zon, 'but I do not see a means of opening it.'

Brad took a look and gave it a push; the door slab of what looked like solid rock, swung up, exposing a dark passage going off into the distance.

'It must be on a counterweight,' commented Brad, 'but why no lock?'

'Perhaps the door into this room was considered sufficient to deter unwanted visitors,' replied Zon, 'so there was no need for it - I would assume.'

At that moment there was a soft whoosh, and the remains of the coat Brad had touched fell to the floor in a cloud of dust. Hanging on the same peg underneath where the coat had been, was a cylindrical object with a metallic sheen.

'I wonder what that is,' said Brad, 'it has what looks like a glass lens on one end, but I didn't think these people had glass. They don't have proper windows, just holes in the walls to let the light in.'

'I am beginning to think there are two different lots of people here,' said Zon, 'those who live in the building, and those who watch them. Maybe the watchers are a little more advanced, by the look of that cylinder.'

Brad reached up and lifted the cylinder off its peg, turning it over in his hands.

'It's quite heavy for its size,' Brad commented, 'and there's a little knob on the side. Think it's safe to fiddle with it?'

'Point it at the wall over there,' Zon replied, 'it may be a weapon of some kind.'

Brad pointed the cylinder with its glass end at the wall next to the opening they had just found, and pressed the knob - nothing happened.

'I'll try and slide it,' he added.

A beam of intense white light lit up the wall, spilling out to illuminate the whole room. Brad nearly dropped the light emitting device in surprise, and then having recovered from the shock, swung it into the dark hole they had discovered.

'This is what we call a torch,' said Brad, 'batteries power a light emitting device. That tunnel seems to go on forever, and if we go down it and the torch runs out of power, we could be in big trouble. I'll see if there is another one behind the other cloaks.'

The second cloak responded much like the first one, descending in a cloud of dust, revealing another torch, and a sigh of relief from Brad.

'So, what do we do?' asked Brad, 'go back into the main building or down the tunnel to see where it leads?'

'This building was abandoned a very long time ago,' Zon replied, 'I think there is very little left of interest here, so we may as well go down the tunnel and see what lies ahead. We will take the two light devices to be on the safe side. I think you should check your food supplies - how much do you have left?'

Brad dug into his carry bag. There were several fruits and large nuts, along with his concentrates - and for the first time, he realised he was thirsty - very thirsty, and said so.

'We must find water for you,' said Zon, 'eat the fruits only, this will help.'

As they entered the tunnel, the door from the tower swung shut, followed by the stone tunnel door after they had gone in a few metres.

'Whoever built this place certainly had security in mind,' said Brad, as they padded along, 'they left very little to chance.'

The tunnel walls were smooth, as though they had been cut out by a machine, although Brad couldn't envisage what that machine would look like. Using only one torch, the pair strode out at a good pace. As the tunnel sloped gently upwards and after they had gone what Brad thought was about three kilometres, he called a halt - his legs were about to give out, and he sat down on the tunnel floor.

'You must eat more,' said Zon, 'and rest your legs. They are not used to such hard exercise, in time they will grow strong again. I don't think we are far from the end of this passage, I can feel a draft of cool air.' Brad was too busy eating to reply.

At long last, daylight could be seen, and they were soon out of the tunnel - but where were they?

The air was cold, and a steady wind blew grey clouds across the sky. Brad began to shiver.

'How can there be such a big change from where we were to this, in such a short distance?' Brad asked, between chattering teeth. 'Where's all the lava and smoking volcanoes?'

'We have gone quite a distance, and this is on the other side of the mountain range. We are now shielded from the Fire Lands. The watchers must have come this way, so we had better watch out for them - if they still live, which I doubt.'

Before them was a long slope of grey slate-like stone, shattered into small pieces by some unknown force, and stretching off into the far distance below. Brad stepped forward from the small ledge of rock they had come out on, and his feet slid out from under him. Zon's whip like arm extended out in a flash to grab him and haul him back onto the solid rock.

'You cannot walk on that surface, it will slip from under you, and you will gain much speed by the time you reach the bottom - enough to kill you maybe. We must find out how the others moved from here.'

'Thanks, that was a close one,' said Brad, gaining his feet once more, 'how the hell do we get away from here?'

'We shall have to apply a bit of what you call logic to the situation,' Zon replied, 'as there were only four cloaks hanging in the room we left, there is likely to be only four 'watchers', as you call them. As the cloaks were still there, we can assume that the 'watchers', or their remains, are somewhere in the building. They have not returned to their main place of living, wherever that is, and I do not think it is the building we have left. They certainly did not live up here on this ledge, so they must have come up here somehow.'

'If they didn't go back home, surely the others of their group would come looking for them?' said Brad, 'Perhaps they did come, and took all the others back down with them.'

'I somehow do not think that is likely,' Zon said after a moments pause, 'I think they came up here, went down to the building, and something happened to them and the others who lived there. We must find out how they got up onto this ledge, and then we can use the same method to get down.'

They searched the ledge around the entrance of the tunnel, but could find no hint as to how the watchers had got up there - it was just bare rock. Then Brad wandered around a corner at the far end of the ledge, and called out to Zon.

'Come and see this,' he said, 'I think we've found it.' A large pulley wheel mounted in a frame, and anchored into the rock behind, stood there - but there was no sign of a rope or chain, or a winding mechanism.

'Well, that's where they came up and down,' said Brad, 'but there's no sign of what they were in. There must have been something they sat or stood in to be hauled up the slope.'

'I think the travelling device has been dismantled, maybe by the people who lived in the building. Perhaps they discovered they were being watched, and decided to put a stop to it.'

'What if we just lay down on the slope, we could slide down. I know it's a long way down - what do you think?' he asked Zon.

'We would travel too fast for one thing, and we do not know what is at the bottom. I would not risk it in my present form, and I do not think you should either.'

'You said in your present form, do you mean that you could, if you changed into something else?'

'Yes, that is possible. But it might frighten you beyond your comfort.'

'I'm willing to risk it, if you are. I'm beginning to freeze up here.'

'I could take on the form I used to bring you from the crash site, and you could ride on top of me. I could make two extensions that would dig into the shale, so being able to control our speed, and steer a straight course. Are you sure it will not frighten you too much?'

Brad thought for a moment, but could see no other way they could reach the bottom of the slippery shale slope in one piece, and said, 'OK, let's do it.'

'I suggest you lay down on the ledge, and close your eyes until we reach the bottom, and open them when I tell you.'

Brad did as he was bid, shivering even more as the cold rock sucked even more heat from his already chilled body.

Zon no longer looked human as he changed his appearance, forming a shallow boat shape with two fins at the back, and hardening the surfaces. Two pseudopods extended out to lift Brad gently onto its back, curving round to hold his body in place for the ride down the slope. Brad's eyes were tight shut - he didn't want the illusion of a human form to be shattered. It was one of the few things he had to hold onto, in order keep his sanity in this strange land.

Brad could feel Zon's body undulating beneath him as it moved closer to the edge of the drop, and then the falling sensation made him feel sick as the pair accelerated down the slope. At first, there was just a quiet rustle as the flat platelets of shattered shale gave way to the descending bodies, but this was soon replaced by a noisy rattle, gaining in volume as they gained speed, followed by several lurches as Zon corrected their path and reduced speed by digging in the rear pseudopods. Brad wanted to call to Zon, but thought better of it, as it might distract him from steering a safe course.

After what seemed like an interminably long time, the noise grew less, and they slithered to a stop. Brad was gently lifted down and laid on the ground, not daring to open his eyes until told to by Zon.

'You can open your eyes now,' said Zon, having resumed his humanoid figure, 'that was quite exhilarating, but I would not like to do it too often.' he added, jovially.

They had arrived at the bottom edge of the shale slope, where a few withered plants struggled to get a foothold on unforgiving ground. In the distance, a few bushes and clumps of grass fared better, while in the far distance trees reached for the sky on gently sloping hills.

'How fast were we going?' asked Brad.

'I have no means of measuring that,' Zon replied, 'but it was much faster than I can run, and that is fast.'

They looked back to where they had come from and could only just make out the ledge high up on the long slope, and no sign of the hole they had exited the mountain from. Close by, there was a small square block-like building, with a hole high up on one wall. From the hole, a piece of chain dangled down to a huge pile of tangled metal on the ground.

'It looks like someone has disconnected the chain from the top of the slope, and gravity did the rest.' said Zon, 'Whoever did that, did not return here. So why did the others down here not go to their rescue? And where are the remains and buildings of others?'

Brad was rummaging about in his carry bag, looking for something to eat.

'I think we should get you some food stuffs,' said Zon, 'and a drink of water. There should be some fruit bearing trees over there,' pointing to the distant tree line.

'Where are we going now?' asked Brad, as they set off towards the trees, 'you did mention a cold zone, all ice and snow - can we go there?'

'We could, but you would not survive very long as you do not have enough coverings, and that is something I can not make for you. I would suggest we head for the mountain top I saw up in the tower.

I know that area well, and there is much to see there. Do you agree?'

'Whatever you say,' replied Brad, 'it's all new to me.'

Once they had pushed their way through the line of grassy tufts and bushes, the trees came into full view, and Zon set about pointing out those fruits which were good to eat. Brad ate his fill, and then the search for water began.

Chapter 3
Dangerous water

'You see that line of footprints?' said Zon, 'Those have been made by many different animals, so if we follow them, I would expect us to find water.'

'I can't see any footprints,' said Brad, 'the ground is covered in some sort of grass.'

'Look closely, the grass has been pressed down by their weight. Trust me, I have seen this before.'

Zon led the way through the trees, and down a gentle slope to a rocky area where a pool of crystal-clear water was glinting in the sunlight.

'Would it be alright for me to bathe in that water after I've had a good drink?' Brad asked, 'I feel dusty, and not very clean after all that heat in the Fire Lands; and I would like to wash my clothes'

'I would suggest not in this pool. I have noticed your body is not like mine, and it would leave a scent in the water. Let us find another one, without animal tracks around it. There should be others here.'

'I've found a place,' said Brad, a few minutes later, 'and the grass isn't trampled flat, so nothing is using it for drinking.' Soon he was stripped down to his skin, and was about to plunge in, when Zon grabbed his arm to stop him.

'There must be a reason why nothing drinks here,' Zon said, 'let me see if it is safe for you.' He picked up a long thin stick and dangled it in the water. A few seconds later, and the stick was almost pulled from his grasp by a set of jaws, with a set of very business-like teeth.

'It's like a thing we call an eel. It might give me a nip, but it's not dangerous.' Brad said, seeing his wash being put on hold.

'Look deep into the water,' Zon responded, 'the head is only small, but look deeper and you will see a very large body, much bigger than yours. If you could not get away from the mouth, it could pull you down and eat you at its leisure. Just because a thing looks like something from your world, it does not mean it is the same. Let us find another pool.'

A few minutes later, they found a small pool surrounded by rocks, and Zon pronounced it safe to enter. Brad was surprised to find he didn't feel any embarrassment being naked in front of his companion, and after his wash, did the same for his clothes. A few minutes running about to get dry, much to the amusement of Zon; with his clothes hanging from nearby bushes to dry, he felt refreshed and ready for the next stage of their discovery.

They walked on down the valley, and then climbed a small hill so that Zon could get his bearings on the mountain he had seen from the tower.

'That is what we must head for, and then I will be on ground that I know on the other side of it.' said Zon, 'But on this side of the mountain I have never been, so we must be careful.'

They had only gone a few hundred metres, when a plaintive squeal could be heard.

'Something is in pain,' said Zon, 'I must see if I am needed.'

They followed the sound and came across a jumble of rocks, from which the sound was coming. Three Rockcats were perched on top of the rocks in an agitated state, looking down into a deep cleft. At the bottom of the cleft was a Rockcat lying at an awkward angle, and mewing softly.

'It must have slipped and got jammed in that crevice,' said Zon, 'I will extend my arm and try to release it. Look away, if my doing this will disturb you.'

Zon's right arm grew into a long thin rope-like structure, and slid down to where the Rockcat lay trapped. Brad looked on, still not used to the morphing abilities of his friend and suppressed a gulp as the extension grew three fingers and gently wrapped themselves around the Rockcat, lifting it free from the entrapping cleft.

'I think a leg has been twisted out of joint,' Zon said, 'I must put it in its right place.'

One of the fingers tapped the Rockcat on the head, and it went limp. Zon deftly realigned the joint, stroked the back of the Rockcat's head, and laid it down on a flat area of rock. Slowly the eyes opened, and the Rockcat assumed its usual smile. The tender care shown by Zon brought a lump up in Brad's throat, and he wondered just what else this strange creature was capable of. The other Rockcats gathered around their injured companion, mewing away and stroking it, while Brad and Zon backed away from the little group.

'If you hadn't come along, what would have happened to the cat?' asked Brad.

'It would have sadly died,' replied Zon, 'one of its legs was trapped in the rocks and had been twisted out of joint so it could not escape. I do not think its companions could have released it.'

They continued on down the hill to a deep valley, where the trees grew tall and thin with garlands of creepers hanging down, most of which were festooned with multi-coloured flowers. As they walked between them, Brad suddenly felt dizzy and staggered up against a tree. The flowering vines above him bent their blooms down, and a fine, barely visible perfumed mist descended. Zon realised that Brad had stopped, and returned to him, slipping an arm under his, and dragged him away from the tree.

'I think you must be susceptible to the smell of those flowers,' he said, 'we must hurry away from here before you go to sleep.'

As the trees petered out, they came to a clearing at the bottom of the valley, and Brad sat down on the grass to rest, his head still swimming from the perfumed flowers.

'What was that all about?' asked Brad, 'It was a very pleasant smell, but I nearly went to sleep.'

'If you noticed, around the tree bases there were some little white sticks. I think they were the remains of bones from animals which were overwhelmed by the smell. It is the tree's way of getting food - not pleasant, but effective; as I said, we must be very careful, as I do not know the hazards this area may have.'

They left the clearing, and began the long climb up the next hill, pausing every now and again as Brad plucked fruits from the trees they passed, eating some and stocking up his carry bag. So far, he hadn't eaten any of his concentrates since leaving the pool where his body had lain recuperating, and he begun to miss the flavour of meat.

A deep-toned hum filled the air as they came to an upthrust of rocks, the ground all around them devoid of vegetation.

'Where is that noise coming from?' asked Brad, looking around, 'It's too deep for insects, and I haven't noticed many of them anyway.'

'If you look up, you will see what is making that hum.' said Zon, 'It's what you would refer to as bees, but they are much bigger than the ones in your memory. I think we should retreat from here, as they do not know your smell, and may attack if they think you are a threat to them.'

High above their heads, flying creatures the size of a clenched fist wove among the flowering trees, some going down to the cluster of rocks and disappearing from view for a while, then returning to continue their nectar gathering.

Several hills were climbed before the mountain came fully into view, and when it did it was a magnificent sight. Great slabs of rock jutted out from the main core, dark and menacing, looking like a barrier far too arduous to climb. But Zon increased his pace, as if he would enjoy the challenge.

As they came to the first outthrust, Zon stopped and looked up at the towering block of stone.

'I think we shall have to use what you would call 'unusual methods' to climb this,' he said, 'it will be far too difficult for you to manage on your own.'

Brad stood there, staring at the sheer rock face, and wondering just what Zon had in mind - he didn't have long to wait.

Zon extended his arms into a rope-like structure, as he had done before, but this time they went far beyond what Brad thought possible, as they snaked up the rock face, finger like extensions appearing at their ends as they groped around trying to find any small crevice to lock into. And then the arms contracted, hauling the figure of Zon up the sheer rock wall.

'There is a small ledge up here where you can rest - you will not be able to see it from there,' he added, 'I will anchor myself to the rock, and then haul you up.'

The arms extended again, to drop down next to Brad, and he gulped in anticipation of what was about to happen. Zon's extensions took a firm grip on Brad's arms, tightened, and he was on his way up. There was just enough room for Brad to place his feet next to his companion's on the narrow ledge, and was then instructed to insert his fingers into any small cracks he could find.

'Just hold yourself flat up against the rock, I will release you and then go up the next section.' Brad had never felt so vulnerable in his long life, and felt sweat break out, and run down his back like icy fingers.

Zon repeated the process several more times, and then they were on top of the huge outcrop, Brad trembling from exertion and fear.

'From the top above us we will see lands I have travelled before, but not all of them have been explored fully, so there may be a few surprises in store for us.'

Brad thought there was grin on Zon's face, but maybe it was just his way of showing confidence in what they were about to do.

More outcrops were climbed using Zon's extending arms, and at long last, much to Brad's relief, they reached the top. Below, rolling hills and valleys stretched away into the distance, with a line of high mountains in the distant background.

'Now we can go down to an area I know a little about. It should be a lot easier than the climb up,' said Zon, and Brad heaved a sigh of relief.

Zon was right, the journey down the mountain was a lot easier than the nerve-wrenching climb up. There were plenty of small streams to drink from and copious amounts of fruit and berries, Zon pointing out new ones which Brad hadn't tried before, much to his delight.

They had nearly reached the base of the mountain when they came across a large flat area of bare stone. It looked as if it had been cut out of the surrounding rock by some unimaginable machine, so flat and smooth was the surface, extending some fifty metres in length and half as wide.

'This can't be the work of nature,' said Brad, 'it's too perfect, and it's certainly not cut by hand tools.'

'I have only seen something like this up by the deep caves,' Zon replied, 'but I do not know what it is used for. It must have a purpose, because of the work needed to make it.'

'It could be a landing place for a space vehicle, but you would probably have noticed it, or at least come across the people from it.' said Brad.

'I am beginning to think my world has been visited by more people that I thought,' Zon said, 'although there is plenty of life here, I assumed I was the only one with real intelligence and thought - it looks as if I was wrong. You will see some more strange things when we visit the deep caves, although at the time, I gave little thought to it.'

They scoured the flat area for clues but found nothing except some deep round holes drilled around the periphery of the rocky platform, but that didn't help much, except that something other than animals had been around here.

The pair left the enigmatic platform and continued their journey down to where the ground levelled out to an area of sand and gravel, on which nothing grew. They were just about to step onto it, when again, Zon put out a restraining hand.

'There is something not quite right here,' he said, 'I can feel it.'

'What do you mean?' said Brad, 'It looks like similar ground we have gone over before.'

'Give me one of your fruits.' Zon held out his hand, and then threw the plum shaped fruit into the middle of the sandy area, next to a large dead leaf, no doubt blown there by the wind. It lay there for a few moments, and then the sand around it trembled and the fruit slowly sank out of sight.

'It is similar to the sinking sands. But why did the leaf not sink? It is just as well we did not walk onto it, we shall have to go around.'

'Wait a moment,' said Brad, 'I'd like to try something.'

Brad went back to where a tree sported large leaves, and pulled two off, wrapping one leaf around a small stick to give it weight, and threw it high into the air over the centre of the sands. As the bundle descended, the leaf uncurled and fluttered down to the sandy surface, the stick carrying on to land some distance away, the leaf just laying there. Brad then took the other leaf, bit into one of his fruits and smeared its juice onto the leaf. Taking another stick, he wrapped the leaf around it and also threw it out over the sand. This time, a few moments after the leaf landed, a thin tentacle broke the surface, wrapped itself around the leaf and both disappeared below the surface.

'Now we know what's hiding in those sands,' said Brad, trying not to look too pleased with himself, 'there might well be bigger ones down there, big enough to take us down.'

'You have reasoned that out well,' said Zon, 'together we should survive well.'

'Thank you,' said Brad, 'I am surprised you haven't come across this sort of thing before, as you said you had been here a very long time.'

'It is a very big world, and I have a lot more to explore. Some places do not feel right, so I avoid them. I can not foresee a situation where I would lose my life, except if I fell into a red-hot liquid rock pool - you call it a volcano.'

They walked around the deadly sands, and continued their journey up the next hill, only pausing to pick the odd fruit which Brad found hard to resist. Suddenly, the ground under their feet shuddered, and they stopped in their tracks.

'This happened when we were at the pool after your crash,' said Zon, 'and it has happened several times before. What do you think it is?'

'Do you have mountains in long chains, stretching over a great distance?' asked Brad, 'I don't mean just the odd one on its own.'

'Yes, there are several in this area, and many more a long way from here near the great sea.'

'To put it simply, most worlds have what are called tectonic plates, which make up the lithosphere, the outermost layer of a world. This is made up of the upper crust, which we are walking on now, and a lower layer which is pliable to a degree. Forces within the world cause these plates to move over a long period of time. When one plate pushes up against another one, sometimes the forces are great enough to make one plate bunch up, so forming a ridge - that is your mountain range, but it does take an awful lot of time to form. If one plate is pushed underneath another one, and is forced down, that is called a subduction zone, the friction causes it to melt, and if there is a weakness near the surface, it will force the liquid rock up. That is what we call a volcano - your Fire Lands is a good example of this. Did you notice flashes of light about the time of the shudders, especially when it was dark?'

'Yes, I often wondered why. They only appear in certain places, and sometimes there are balls of light floating about for a short time,' Zon answered.

'The two things are linked,' Brad replied, 'Certain minerals, especially quartz, when they are stressed sharply, emit what we call electrons - energy partials - and when they reach the surface they show as a flash of light. A sudden plate movement is enough to compress the quartz sharply, hence the release of energy.'

'But what makes the shuddering we sometimes feel?' asked Zon.

'When the plates move, it is not always in one easy go. Sometimes a plate, or part of a plate will stick, and then suddenly give way as the forces equalize themselves out - that is the shudder we feel.'

'So, it is not harmful then?' said Zon.

'Only if you are in an area where a volcano bursts out, or near a fault zone which suddenly moves - that can cause loose rocks to tumble about, and trees to fall.'

They continued to walk on up the hill, and having reached the top, looked down on an area of jumbled rocks - what looked like an impassable barrier to their progress.

'I think there may be a way through,' said Zon, screwing his eyes up, 'it looks as if some of those rocks over there have been cut - but I can not be sure from this distance.' Brad couldn't see a way through, but then he didn't have Zon's eyes.

They walked along the top of the jumble of rocks until a hesitant Zon held up his hand.

'This is what I mean by cut rocks,' he said, 'some thing has removed them, making a passage down through to the bottom of the hill.'

Sure enough, the rocks had been sheered off at ground level in a straight line, leaving a clear way down for the two travellers - but neither was keen to step onto this unusual pathway.

'This must have been done by those who used the lifting mechanism to go up the slate hill,' said Brad, 'it's in line with the path we took from there - but there's something about it I don't feel comfortable with.'

'I sense it too,' Zon replied, 'if you look, there is just enough space between the shorn off rocks to place our feet - if we are careful. I think it unwise to actually touch the rock surface, but I do not now why. I will take a small step to see what effect it has.'

Zon put one foot on the top of a sheered off rock, and withdrew it immediately.

'I felt a tingle in my foot,' he said, 'I think it is another way of preventing anything alive from going down that way. The rocks themselves are a barrier, and the people who cut this passageway have kept it so.'

'Those damn rocks go all around the hill, except for where we came up, so we'll have to go down that way.' Brad said, wondering what effect the rocks would have on him.

'I could change the material on the bottom of my feet into something which will not let the tingle effect me,' Zon offered, 'and then I could carry you on my back.'

Zon modified the material of his feet, put one on a rock and promptly took it off again. After several tries, he stood with both feet on the flat surface of the rock, turned to Brad, and gave a grin.

'Jump up on my back, I think we will get through now. But do not touch any rock on either side.'

Once again, Brad did as he was bid, and the pair carefully walked down the pathway, stepping from rock to rock - and then they were out on normal ground again.

'Why did you go from rock to rock? There was some space between them that you could have walked on?' asked Brad.

'Maybe you did not notice, I did put my foot on the ground between the rocks, and I noticed a spark go from the rock to my foot - and it hurt. Whoever wanted to stop anything going down there covered all possibilities.'

A small stream provided Brad with a good drink, and they were on their way again, climbing the next hill. From the top they looked down on another small rise in the ground, and just past it, another hill, on top of which they could see what looked like the remains of several buildings, just the low walls remaining.

'Now that looks interesting,' said Brad, 'we have more habitation. Maybe it's where the watchers lived - I think that's worth a look at.' Zon just nodded, as usual.

As they climbed the far hill with the ruins on its top, it became evident that the remains were far larger than they had thought, and when they actually arrived at the site, they were in for another surprise.

Although only low walls remained, the rest of the buildings had been reduced to shattered rock. Heaps of small stones were all that was left of massive building blocks, some of which were scattered some way from the buildings themselves.

'One hell of a lot of force must have been used here,' said Brad, 'I can't think of anything in my world that could do that. The stone blocks have been ground down to dust almost. If explosive missiles had been used, there would be the odd crater around here, but there aren't any - it's almost as if the blocks themselves had blown up.'

They walked around the ruins, looking for any clues which might explain what had happened, when Brad came across what he thought looked like a skull, tucked in the corner of what had once been a room.

'It looks like a skull,' said Brad, 'but I've never seen one quite like this, it's got a pointed top.'

'It has all the features of those heads we saw in your monastery, except for that strange bump on top.' said Zon, 'If these were the watchers, then they must have been a different people to those we saw earlier.'

'You mean two different races?' asked Brad. Zon nodded.

'Then who blew them to pieces? It can't be the monastery people, they were basically simple people.'

Zon was too preoccupied to answer - he had spotted something in the distance, and was refocusing his eyes to get a better view.

'There is something on top of that hill, which looks different to everything else,' he said, pointing into the far distance, 'I think we should go and have a look at it.'

They set out in the direction Zon had indicated, sleeping overnight in a sheltered hollow, but it wasn't until midday before they came across the next mystery.

'And what the hell is that?' exclaimed Brad, looking up at a collection of grey metal machinery. A huge parabolic shaped saucer, some ten metres in diameter, was poised on top of a sturdy metal frame, below which was barrel shape mass with a short stub of a tube at its end - pointing in the direction of the ruins they had left the day before.

Three supports leaned out from the edge of the saucer shape, joining together to hold a squat cylinder, from which a tube as thick as a man's arm drooped down to the barrel shape below.

'Now this does look like a weapon,' said Brad, confidently, 'but nothing like anything I've seen before. Although that dish shape looks dull now, I bet it was shiny once upon a time - it's a sort of mirror, I would think.'

Zon went over the barrel shape below the dish, inspecting it very carefully.

'I think this portion is meant to move,' he said, 'there is a handle on it.' He tried to lift the cover, but it didn't move.

'Let me have a go,' said Brad, 'perhaps we have to twiddle something to release it first.

Brad found the release catch, and a whole section on the side of the barrel shape lifted up.

'That's the biggest crystal I've ever seen,' he exclaimed, 'my God it's huge, and a pale green colour… this rings a bell.' he added.

'What do you mean, rings a bell? I hear nothing.' Zon looked perplexed.

'I mean it reminds me of something I've seen before. It's called a laser - a means of concentrating light, and letting it out in one almighty burst - very powerful. But what's a laser doing out here? None of these people we've come across have the necessary technology to make something like this.'

'Could it be used as a weapon?' asked Zon, trying to make sense of something he had never heard of.

'Let me check a few things out.' Brad replied, that dish could reflect sunlight into the cylinder thing just in front of it, and that tube thing could be some sort of optical fibre, transferring the light down to the crystal in the barrel. If I remember right, light can be pumped into a crystal where it bounces back and forth, gaining energy until it bursts out of the end. By the size of that dish, that's one hell of a lot of energy.'

'It is pointing in the right direction to destroy the ruins we saw. Do you think it would still work?' asked Zon.

'We could give it a try,' said Brad, 'but the dish is a bit dull, so we won't get full power from it.'

Brad found the lever which moved the dish into alignment with the sun, blazing in a cloudless sky, and then found that using a looped handle on the end of the barrel shape, he could aim the device using two sighting rings on top of the weapon.

'Nothing's happening,' said Brad, 'it must have corroded over time, and now won't work.'

'Try that little lever there,' said Zon, pointing with a finger, 'there is also a small stud next to it - that may release the power.'

Brad pushed the lever down, and thought he felt a vibration from within the barrel, but before he could check it out, a small green light lit up next to the stud, and he knew he had power.

'I'll aim at those rocks over there,' he said, 'but I don't expect we'll see much after all this time.'

Brad pressed the stud, and a pencil thin beam of bright light hit the rocks he had aimed at, blowing them to pieces. A cloud of fine rock dust hung over the spot for a moment, before drifting away in the light breeze.

They both stood there, surprised beyond belief.

'I'm not surprised there was not much left of those buildings. I wonder what it would have been like with the mirror new and polished. Also, it looks as if we have a third group of people here,' said Brad, 'the monastery lot, the watchers, and the lot who blew them away. What else are we about to find?'

'I keep finding new things,' Zon replied, 'but nothing like this. I think our next big surprise will be in the caves - the deep ones - if we can get down there.'

'How much further do we have to go?' asked Brad.

'About two days travel, unless we find something else to distract us.' Zon replied, 'It might be a good idea if we cut a couple of poles - once in the caves, we cannot be sure what we might meet.'

As they were about to leave the area, Brad noticed a small shiny rod with a pointed end, lying on the ground by the weapon.

'I wonder what that is?' he said, 'It might come in useful, I'll put it in my bag.' and did so.

Over the next two days, they did find many new things, mainly new to Brad. One thing did frighten Brad though, apart from a particular strong earth tremor. They had just settled down for the night in a clearing, when a large bear-like creature, the size of a horse, entered the clearing and slowly walked up to Zon. Brad thought he was about to lose his companion, when it raised a front leg, and held it out in front of Zon.

Taking the offered foot, Zon examined it carefully, and extruding a pincer-looking device from one finger, removed a large thorn. The creature lowered its foot to the ground, and feeling satisfied with the result, gave Zon's face a lick with a long purple tongue, and then walked off into the night.

'How come that thing recognised you, when you look like me and not your usual self?' asked a shaken Brad.

'I keep telling you, I have no usual shape.' Zon replied, a little impatiently, Brad thought, 'It recognised me, not the body shape I have adopted.'

'You mean you are not the body I see?' a confused Brad replied.

'That is exactly what I mean - I am me, and this is the body I use to go travelling in - much as you did in your spaceship. You are not the ship, but you controlled it.'

It was far too much for Brad to assimilate in one go, and he decided he would question Zon later, when they were in a more relaxed mood. The night passed peacefully, with no more visitors. Next morning, Brad stocked up his carry bag, had a good drink of water, and they were off again.

True to Zon's estimate, they rounded a particularly large rock formation, and there before them was a massive cliff of dark brown rock, reaching up into the morning sky.

'Is this where the caves are?' asked Brad, not seeing any holes in the sheer rock face before them.

'Yes, but you will not see the entrance from here, it is hidden behind a large slab of rock. I only found it because I thought the rock looked out of place somehow, and went to investigate.'

Brad agreed, the rock blocking the entrance to the caves did look a bit out of place on the flat area under the massive cliffs. It looked as if it had been placed there - but by what? It was too large to be moved by anything Brad could think of.

'My food bag is full, but is there water in the caves?' asked Brad, wishing he had some means of carrying water.

'Yes, that is one thing you will have plenty of,' responded Zon, 'and there should be edible things for you too.' Brad didn't like to ask what they were, but feared the worst.

Chapter 4
The deep caves

GOING AROUND THE rock shielding the view of the cave, they saw the actual entrance, a black hole in the cliff face. The first thing Brad did was to look for footprints around the entrance, and to his relief, found none.

'Shall I get a torch out?' asked Brad, peering into the blackness ahead.

'We will not need your light yet,' Zon replied, 'let your eyes get used to the dark, and you will be able to see quite well.'

They stood there, a few metres inside the huge tunnel, and slowly their eyes got accustomed to the low light level and were able to pick out details of the walls after a few minutes, Brad thinking they had once been lava tunnels, but now worn smoother by water.

Side by side, the pair walked down the tunnel, at one point having to go around large lumps of rock which had been dislodged from the roof, and wondering if any more were due to fall.

A few hundred metres in and they could see quite well, the walls glistening in places from water seepage, and little pools of water on the floor of the passage.

'I've just realised,' exclaimed Brad, 'the walls are giving out light. I hadn't noticed it before - the whole place, it just seemed lit - somehow.'

'It is something growing on the walls,' said Zon, 'it took me a while to find that out. If you look closely, you will see very tiny specs of something sticking to the rock - it glows faintly, but there is so much of it, quite a lot of light is made.'

Suddenly the passage dipped, and they were on their way down well below ground level, when the air took on a damp feeling. The constant drip, drip of water now added to their footfalls as they entered a huge bulge in the tunnel, the cave opening out into a circular shape with the walls draped in curtains of reformed dissolved rock.

They had to wind their way between massive columns of stalagmites rising up from the wet floor, formed over the ages from the dissolved rock above, while stalactites hung down in festoons to meet them, wet and glistening in the gentle light from the surrounding walls.

Brad stopped to admire one particular group, some were colour stained with dissolved minerals as the water seeped down through various layers of metallic bearing ores.

As they left the cave, the passage turned to the left, and the incline down grew steeper. Brad wondered just how far down into the bowels of the planet they were going to go, when they entered a cave, the likes of which Brad couldn't have imagined.

A mass of what looked like tangled roots from some giant tree barred their way, a pale grey in colour and as thick as the top of his leg. Without thinking, Brad gave one of the twisted roots a tap with his stave, and the whole mass trebled, emitting a high-pitched singing sound.

'What the hell is that?' he enquired, stepping back in surprise, 'It feels and looks like stone, so how come it can move like that?'

'I think the outside is hard,' replied Zon, 'but the inside may be flexible. There are several such caves down here, and one where it looks as if the creature has died - the branches are broken and lying in a heap. It has never harmed me when I came down here a long time ago, so we should be able to push through safely. If you notice, the floor is covered with fine sand. I think the creature grows by absorbing the stone in the walls, so enlarging its living space and leaving behind the glass-like sand it cannot use.'

By gently pushing the strange roots, they slowly gave way, and they were out of the cave and into the continuation of the tunnel again.

'We will soon come to the lake,' said Zon, 'I suggest we take a rest, and you can eat something.'

A half kilometre on, and the tunnel opened out into an enormous cavern, the sides fading out into the distance, and the roof out of sight in the soft light. Before them was a lake of still water, and a sandy shore with the odd pebble lying on the surface.

'This will amuse you.' Zon said, picking up a smooth brown pebble, and throwing it far out over the still water. As the pebble hit the surface there was a flash of pale blue light, and as the ripples moved out in a circle, the crest of each ripple briefly flashed the same pale blue.

'What on earth causes that?' asked Brad.

'Nothing on earth,' Zon replied 'I think it is due to very, very small creatures which live in the water. When they are disturbed, they emit light. Dip your hand in the water and wriggle it about, you will get the same effect.'

Brad did so, and the even the water clinging to his hand glowed, but the light emitters were far too small for him to see.

'I would have thought that if they emit light, it would attract other creatures to attack and eat them. I assume there are other creatures in the water?'

'You may be right, but I think it is the other way around - the light level in here is really very low, so if they emit light, it might frighten others away. And yes, there are other creatures in the lake, but I do not think you would like to meet them.' Brad knew better than to argue with his friend, so let the matter drop.

Just then they could see a large blue wave in the distance, cleaving its way towards them, and leaving a foaming pale blue wake.

'I think we had better retreat to the back of the sand line, that creature is a lot bigger than either of us, and I have seen it before. Last time I had to change my skin to a hard stone like substance very quickly because I let it get close enough to bite me. It broke two teeth off in the process.'

As they stepped back from the water's edge, a large head reared out of the lake with its mouth open - and two missing front teeth. Two red eyes glared in their direction, blinked twice, and then the creature slowly sank back into the water - which glowed a beautiful pale blue.

'Could it have got out onto the sand?' asked Brad, stepping back until he hit the wall of the cave.

'I do not know, it may have legs. I did not stay long enough to find out.' said Zon, with what Brad thought was a chuckle in his voice, 'I think we should move on now, that is the passage we need to go down,' he said, pointing to a small dark opening a few metres away.

As they were about to enter, Brad noticed a mass of what looked like pieces of thick string, about fifty centimetres apart, hanging down from the cave roof and stopping just short of the water by about thirty centimetres. The strands slowly wavered in the light air currents which drifted around the cave, and then, one by one, they grew in length, and dipped into the water.

'Have you seen that before?' asked Brad, pointing, 'it looks as if it's alive.'

'It is,' said Zon, 'keep watching, it may take a few moments before you see any action.'

The pair stood with their backs to the cave wall, waiting for what looked like a bunch of strings to do something amazing - and then one did. A strand swiftly rose from the water and retreated up into the gloom overhead, its end firmly wrapped around a little fish-like creature, which was desperately wriggling to free itself, but failed.

Shortly afterwards, another strand left the water on its way up to whatever clung to the cave roof, but this time the captured creature was bigger, and equipped with a fine set of teeth. Reaching around, it severed the strand, and dropped back into the water. The severed strand then oozed thick blobs of a yellowish liquid which dropped into the water below to be gulped up hungrily by a shoal of little swimmers - and then all was quiet again.

'What sort of creature is up on the cave roof?' asked Brad.

'I do not know,' Zon replied, 'I can not see that far up in the gloom, but they are efficient fishers.'

All the hanging strands had now retreated a short distance from the water's surface, and as nothing else happened for a while, they turned from the lake and entered the dark tunnel ahead.

'You should put a hand on my shoulder, and I will guide you through this section,' said Zon, 'there is very little light here, but I can just see, and you will not be able to.'

Zon was right, it was pitch black as far as Brad was concerned, and narrow, so he clung tightly to Zon's shoulder for the next fifty metres or so, and then the tunnel opened out and the gentle glow they were so used to, returned.

A trickle of water ran down the wall to be absorbed by the pumice like floor, and Zon suggested Brad take a drink, after putting a finger in it and pronouncing it safe. After resting a few minutes, they resumed their trek, Zon pointing out various glittering gemstones embedded in the tunnel walls, and again asking why Brad's people valued them so much.

'We will soon see something I do not understand,' said Zon, 'it is a strange pit with a liquid at the bottom, and a very bad smell.'

The pit turned out to be a very deep shaft about five metres wide, with a swirling bubbling dark green fluid seething about at its base. Brad felt compelled to go to the brim and peer down - and then he felt the urge to jump into the hole. There was something nice down there, just for him. He took another step forward, one foot half over the edge, when the restraining hand of Zon gripped his shoulder in a vice-like grip.

'I felt it too,' said Zon, 'but only a little. It must be a living force of some kind because it reached your mind, and only a living thing can do that.'

Brad stepped back from certain death, and broke into a sweat.

'Now that was really nasty,' he said, 'I knew it was dangerous, but

there was an overwhelming feeling that I would be alright, and I
wanted to jump in'

'If you have a soft fruit, throw it in,' Zon suggested, 'it would be
interesting to see what happens to it.'

Brad dug into his food bag and withdrew a large black plum-like
fruit, and lobbed it into the middle of the swirling pool. As it hit the
surface, the liquid shrank back from it, and then rose in a thin wall
around the plum to enclose it - and the plum was no more - except for
a small puff of water vapour which slowly drifted up the shaft.

'Whatever is down there it is very hot,' said Brad, 'hot enough to boil
the water from the fruit. But I don't see how it can be a living thing, at
that temperature.'

'And yet it seems to be, it touched your mind,' from Zon.

They left the pit with its mind-altering powers, and continued on
down another steep slope, the walls of which had turned colour to a
pale purple, which Brad found uncomfortable to his eyes. Zon halted
at a side tunnel, and indicated that they should go in. After a few
metres, they were in an enormous cavern which seemed to blaze with
light. From below them, massive crystals of some transparent mineral
grew from the floor to reach almost to the level at which they stood.

'I have never seen crystals of that size,' said an astonished Brad, 'they
must be at least a metre across and six metres long - and they look
wet.'

'If we wait a while, we may see why they look wet,' said Zon, 'I saw
it last time when I was down here.'

They stood at the edge of the huge pit, and waited. Brad was all for
returning to the main tunnel after a while, but Zon put a restraining
arm on his. A soft rushing noise could be heard as a fluid slowly rose
to engulf the mass of crystals, and then receded, leaving the crystals
glistening wet.

'I think the liquid has something in it which the crystals use to
grow,' said Zon, 'but they are all without colour, except two over there,
and they are pale green like the one in the weapon we saw. Shine a
torch on them, something may happen.'

Brad took a torch from his carry bag, switched it on, and aimed it at
a crystal - but nothing happened.

'These crystals are six sided and have a point at the end, the one in
the laser was round and with flat ends - it has to be for it to laze - the
light has to bounce back and forth until it builds up so much that it
breaks out of one end to form the light beam. Someone has some very

sophisticated equipment to cut a crystal of that size,' he added.

They left the crystal cave, but had to wait a few minutes for their eyes to get used to the lower light level in the tunnel before proceeding.

'We are not far from the deep caves I told you about,' said Zon, 'but there is one more thing I would like to show you first.'

As they walked along, Brad saw that the tunnel was not quite the same as those they had travelled earlier.

'This section looks different,' he said, 'it looks as if it has been machined out, instead of the normal roughness on the walls we had before.'

Zon stopped and closely examined the walls.

'I think you are right,' he said, 'I had not noticed it before. Maybe the people who used the crystal weapon made this section so that they could get at the crystals, which means they came from below here, as we are going down all the time.'

Another hundred metres, and they came to a cave of enormous proportions - and before them was a vast forest of what looked to Brad like giant mushrooms. They towered over the pair as they walked in amongst them, the stems a full half metre wide, and the tops of the tallest ones disappearing in the gloom overhead.

'The big ones are quite hard,' said Zon, 'and you would not be able to eat them. But the very small ones should still be soft. I will test one for you.' And he drove a finger into one, withdrew it, and pronounced it good to eat.

Brad was a little doubtful about adding them to his diet, as they looked so alien, but Zon had always been right in the past. He broke a small portion off a small one growing at his feet, and hesitatingly took a small bite.

'Hey, this is good,' Brad said, 'it's a bit nut-like in flavour - and the texture is good. Thanks, I'll put a few in my bag.'

'One thing I don't understand,' said Brad, 'is if the people who made the laser got the crystal from down here, how did they get it up to the surface? We have been through several places which would have been too narrow for them, we only just got through.'

'Perhaps you did not notice, but near the entrance the tunnel divided in two - the lit one we went down, and another one which was off to one side, and not well lit. I came up it last time I was down here.'

A few more caves on each side of the tunnel held odd plant growths, and Brad couldn't understand how they could grow in such poor light. One even had a beautiful deep red bloom on it, with a set of waving yellow stamens in the middle, and Brad questioned the reason for a flower deep inside the earth.

'Take a quick smell of it,' said Zon, 'and that will answer your question, and then look at the base of the plant.'

Brad did - and felt dizzy in seconds. Where the plant sent its roots down into what seemed to be solid rock, a cluster of small bones littered the floor. Zon's arm gently led Brad away to the entrance of the cave, and told him to take deep breaths.

After staggering along for a few metres, Brad gradually regained his normal walking gait, and after turning a corner on the downward slope, Zon stopped dead in his tracks.

'I am getting that feeling again - that I must not go any further,' said Zon in a worried voice, 'It is very strong. I will take a few more steps. It is stronger now, and my legs feel weak.'

'That's odd,' Brad replied, 'I don't feel anything. As we haven't seen any actual people here, I think it must be something mechanical, or electronic, set up to stop you and nobody else - otherwise they couldn't get down here. Are you sure you can't override it?'

Zon took another few faltering steps, and almost collapsed.

'I must go back a few paces,' he said, 'I can sense something awful, but I do not know what it is.'

'OK, let's use a bit of logic,' Brad said, 'There must be something in the area sending out the feelings just for you. If I can find it, we may be able to disable it, and then we can go on. Anyway, you said it had to be a living thing to touch your mind - I suspect it is mechanical, and sends out a vibration which resonates with something in you, so you are affected by it.' Zon didn't look very convinced.

Brad scoured the tunnel walls, and then went a few metres on, still looking for anything unusual, meanwhile Zon had retreated several metres back up the tunnel, to where he felt less threatened.

'I think I've found something,' Brad shouted, 'there are four metal mounts set in the tunnel wall, and each has a small crystal set in the middle of it. They are set back at an angle so you can't see them as you approach - clever! They aren't giving out any light or anything. If I can break them free, that may disable them.'

'Be careful,' Zon called back, 'they may be like the crystal we found in that weapon, and that could injure you.'

Brad rummaged about in his carry bag to retrieve the metal rod he had picked up earlier by the laser weapon, and having found it, gave one of the crystals a sharp tap.

Nothing untoward happened, so he took a real swing at it, and the crystal shattered. 'Right, that's one down, and three more to go,' he called out cheerfully, 'nothing happened except a small shower of broken crystal bits. That's odd, when they hit the ground, the little bits seem to repel themselves from each other - a bit like two north poles of a couple of magnets.'

Soon all four crystals had been removed from their mounts, leaving the shattered remains lying on the floor of the tunnel.

'Try coming forward now,' Brad called out, and Zon took a few hesitating steps forward, and then broke into a run to join his companion.

'That was clever of you,' he said, 'I would not have thought of that, and I do not think I could have got close enough to them to do what you did.'

Brad idly scuffed a few shards of crystal with his foot into a pile, and they promptly spread out again, as if being in contact with each other was abhorrent to them.

'Well, if that isn't the damnedest thing,' Brad exclaimed, 'this place is full of surprises.'

Now that they were able to proceed on down the passage. Ahead, the tunnel came to a stop. Their way was blocked by a sheet of what looked like metal, dull grey in colour, and heavily built.

'I don't see any means of opening it,' said Brad, after a cursory glance, 'I don't think they want us in there,' giving the door a good kick. It rang with a bell-like tone.

'I doubt it will be locked, probably a simple catch,' Zon added, 'there would be little need for a complicated lock down here. Those crystals were all that was needed to keep me out, so who else, apart from those who dwell here, would want to get in?'

'Just thought of something else,' said Brad, 'why would they make something to keep just you out? You must have existed here while they were doing whatever they did, and they knew about you.'

Together they explored the door, but no opening mechanism could be found, much to their frustration. It was Zon who found the means of opening it.

'Look, there is a bar running along the bottom of the door, and I do not see what purpose it has,' he put a foot on it, 'I think I felt a small movement, add some of your weight.'

With their combined weights, the bar dropped a centimetre into a recess, and the door obligingly slid to one side. Ahead, things looked different. One by one, rod-like luminaries in the ceiling of the tunnel flickered into life, and the tunnel was different, a square section, and smooth.

'What happens if we can't open the door on the way out?' asked Brad, thinking ahead.

'If you noticed,' Zon replied, 'the bar we trod on extends right under the door to the other side. We can try it, if you wish.' Brad was annoyed he hadn't spotted it.

A few metres down the passage they found a door set in the wall. They looked at each other.

'Why not?' said Brad, 'that's what we're here for.'

This door was smaller, and the bar at its base only needed Brad's heavy foot to open it. Inside was long room, the lights coming on automatically as they entered.

'My God, it's a machine shop,' exclaimed Brad, 'but I don't recognise any of the machines. Wait a minute, that one over there looks like a drilling machine.'

Zon looked puzzled, and Brad had to explain what a drilling machine did.

A laser or plasma cutter, Brad wasn't sure which, was explained along with several other devices, but most of the other machines were beyond his comprehension.

'With a workshop like this, you could make just about anything,' Brad said, 'but there's no sign of anything they have actually made. Looks like they finished what they were doing, and just left. One thing I don't understand is how come the power plant is still working,' and then had to explain what a power plant was, 'there must be one here somewhere, and that's what I'd like to see,' he added.

They left the machine shop and found another door, a little further down the passage. This one produced clear blocks of what Brad thought were plastic, but when he examined one closely, it proved not to be so, more like glass - and then he realised it was hollow.

'There's a whole stack of them over there,' he said, pointing at the end of the room, 'and they're all different sizes. Wonder what they used them for?' Zon shrugged as usual when he had nothing to offer in reply.

Many other rooms were discovered, but most were beyond their understanding, and they were left trying to figure out just what the complex was for.

'This place could make just about anything you could think of,' said Brad, 'yet there's no sign of anything they've made on the surface - except the monastery place, the ruins, that laser gun thing, and the weapon, the other things don't seem like these people made them. Have you come across anything they've made in your travels?'

'No, nothing I recognised as manufactured, except the things we found together., They could have made them, if they wished to.' replied Zon.

'Let's try this room,' said Brad, stamping his foot down harder than was necessary on the door opening bar.

Several odd-looking machines lay in a line down the middle of the room, while shelves with transparent boxes lined the walls. Brad walked up to one box and stopped short.

'I don't like the look of this,' he said, 'this is spooky. The box is full of what look like little bones, and they're all the same. Why would they kill a whole lot of animals and save the bones?' he asked.

Zon came over to take a look and took a bone out of the box. His fingers curled over the bone, and the hand turned into a round blob before returning to normal, and the bone was placed back in its box.

'They are real bones,' he said, a puzzled look on his face, 'and they are identical. This would not be so if they were taken from real animals, as they grow to slightly different sizes, and the bones would too. I think these bones were made here, as there is no trace of flesh having been on them. But I do not understand how, or why.'

They didn't realise just how big the room was, or how many boxes of bones there were, until they had walked the length of the of the bone store.

Three more rooms were explored, but the contents made little sense to the pair; except one room, where a small piece of what looked like leather, or maybe skin, was left on a tabletop. It had curled up and dehydrated, crumpling into dust when Brad picked it up.

Back in the passageway, and feeling a little uncomfortable, they found it forked off into two, and with Brad in the lead, they took the left-hand turn.

A large metal door barred their way, and there was no foot bar to press down. A strange sign adorned the top of the door, and Brad thought it might be some kind of warning, but didn't know why.

'I think we have another of these combination puzzles,' said Zon, pointing out an odd pattern of studs in the middle of the door, 'as we did before, you press the studs in turn, and I will listen for any sounds they make.'

It took longer than they expected to find the right combination, and were on the point of giving up when there was a loud clunk, and the door swung open. Ahead, a short passage terminated in what could be described as a viewing room, complete with what looked like a massive glass shield from which they looked down on a complicated mass of machinery, in the centre of which lay a huge torus.

'I knew it,' exclaimed Brad excitedly, 'this is the power generator, I knew it had to be here somewhere. That round shape is what we call torus - it's where particles of matter are smashed together at very high speed to form something else, and in doing so release lots of energy. It must have been ticking over in semi shutdown mode until we opened the first door, and then it came up to full power. Must say, it's very small and compact compared to those I know about.'

'I have a feeling that we may look, but not go down into that room. It is only a feeling, but I think I am right.' said Zon.

Reluctantly they left the power generator, and returned to where the passage broke again into two, taking the right hand turn this time. During their explorations, Brad had made several stops for food, mainly soft fruits, and wondered how his companion could go so long without sustenance.

The next room to be investigated was a clue as to what had been happening in the complex, although the pair had not yet joined all the dots up together, so to speak.

This room, with its benches and assembly tables, and other strange looking machines, would have remained a mystery if it had not been for one item left behind by the previous occupants. On one table at the far end, and they nearly missed it, was the complete skeleton of a four-legged creature about the size of a small dog.

They both stood there, spell bound and speechless for a few moments, as the realisation sank in.

'This isn't something being stripped down to its bare bones,' exclaimed Brad, 'it's something being built up! Look, there is one bone missing on its leg, and there it is lying on the table, ready to be attached. But how do they do that?'

'They could use an adhesive, as I do, when something is broken,' offered Zon, 'but I do not see the point of doing so. Why go to all this trouble to assemble a skeleton, when it is easier to take one from an existing creature?'

Brad tried to move one of the creature's legs, and found it articulated as it would have done in real life.

'The bloody thing is jointed,' he almost shouted, 'but this is impossible! A joint is a very complicated thing - I couldn't make one, not one that worked like this.'

'Perhaps that device on your left has something to do with it,' offered Zon, 'it must have a reason for being on the same table, and it looks as if the table's purpose it to assemble things.'

'I don't get it,' Brad replied, 'so they make a skeleton which is fully articulated, but then what do they do with it?

'Maybe if we look in other rooms we may find out,' said Zon, 'there must be a good reason for all this equipment. I do not think it is just to make a model skeleton of an existing creature, it would be far easier to use the real thing. I think we have a lot more to find out.'

They left the assembly room with more questions than when they had entered, but then each room they investigated seemed to have the same effect.

Again, the passageway divided in two, so this time they chose the right hand one, and entered the first room in that section.

Eight tables ran down the centre of the room, with what looked like a conveyor belt against each opposing wall. Each table had two machines on it, but they were different to anything else the pair had yet seen. One had a flexible tube connected to it, which then ran up into the ceiling, while the other one seemed to be enclosed in a transparent box, with a clear door on its front.

Two more rooms, and they were the last in this section of the passageway, had equally mystifying devices in them, and the pair were none the wiser for examining them.

Returning to the junction, they went down the other passage, through the door, and entered a vast space which stretched off into the distance, full of different sized transparent blocks on plinths.

The first set of blocks contained what they thought were insects, all different, but some only in small degrees from the one next to them.

The second row was a little easier to discern. They were obviously aquatic creatures, some almost like the fish Brad had known in the past.

The third row caused most concern, as it contained incredibly realistic reproductions familiar to both of them, creatures they had seen up on the surface.

'Hey, look at this,' Brad cried out, 'it's one of your Rockcats.'

The little creature was sitting up, one paw raised as if in greeting, it's big brown moist eyes smiling out of the cube at its visitors.

Brad thought he heard Zon gulp, but it could have been something else.

'Have you noticed there are no big animals in your world, except that bear-like thing with the thorn in its foot? On my world we have some huge ones.' said Brad.

'Yes, I have seen some of them in your pictures when you were asleep. I do not know why there are none here.'

Eighteen cubes down the row, and they saw the bear creature in its transparent case.

'I am beginning to understand why I was not supposed to come down here - if nothing else, it was to protect my sanity. Let us move on to the last row, over there. I think our questions about this place are to be answered.'

The larger cubes of transparent material at the beginning of the row held some odd-looking humanoid shapes; they had two legs, two arms, a head, and a trunk, but there the resemblance to a human being ended. Brad thought they were grotesque, and said so. A few blocks down, and there was a gasp from both of them.

'This one has the head like the ones we saw in the monastery place,' said Zon in a hushed voice, 'I know we only saw the heads, but now we know what the bodies look like.'

And then they came to some humanoids with pointed heads, short, tall, and some with elongated arms.

'These heads look like the skull we found in the ruins,' said Brad, 'I wonder why they made so many different types?'

'I think I know why,' Zon replied, 'I will tell you if my thoughts prove correct.'

Towards the end of the line, but set aside from the others blocks by a short distance, they came to the greatest revelation of all. Sitting in its case was a grey/brown lump, about two metres long and half a metre high. What looked like a limb sticking up from the middle of the lump, with three fingers on its end.

The next case held a blob shape, but this time it had four stumpy legs, and a rudimentary head with two baleful eyes.

Zon stood transfixed looking at the last cube, and Brad joined him.

Zon's voice was almost a whisper, and Brad thought he was shaking slightly.

'That is what I look like when I am not taking on a shape for a reason. Why have they made a copy of me? I have never seen them, so how did they see me without my knowing?'

Brad rested an arm on Zon's shoulder, somehow knowing he was going through an emotional upheaval, and not knowing what else to do.

'I think we should put all the information we have gathered so far, together. Connect up all the things we think are related to what we have found here, and we may get a better picture about what this whole complex all about, and your part in it,' said Brad quietly, 'I don't think things are quite what they may seem. Come on my friend, I don't think there is much else for us to see down here that will help us. I think we should return to the surface, and take a rest - there is an awful lot to think over, and we can always come down here again if we want to.'

Although Brad would have liked to remain in the complex - searching out new wonders, he realised that Zon's concept of himself was undergoing changes, and he felt it better get out of this environment, and into one a little more predictable and pleasant.

Zon gave a shudder, turned, and followed Brad as he made his way back up the passageways to the big metal door where they had entered the complex. With both putting their weight on the release bar, the door slid back, and they were in the old familiar tunnels.

'This is the easiest way up, along there,' said Zon, pointing to the left-hand passage, and having regained his composure, to some degree.

The tunnel, unlike those they had used on the way down to the complex, was square in section, and machine cut. The walls gave out a little light, but were not as bright as those on the way down, and Brad queried this.

'I would think these passages are newer than those we used earlier, they were natural and could have been here for a very long time' said Zon, 'the growth on these walls has not had time enough to build up, so the light is less.'

They stopped halfway up, for Brad to rest his legs and take on some sustenance, Zon remarking that he must be getting fitter by the day. Little else was said as they climbed up towards the surface, but both were deep in thought about what they had seen.

'This is where we join the main tunnel, quite near the entrance,' said Zon, 'the reason you did not see it on the way down is that it is at an angle, and not very well lit.'

Soon they were out in daylight, the huge overpowering mass of the cliff behind them, and the green world of hills and valleys stretching out before them.

'You must be in need of water,' said Zon, 'I think it is dangerous to deplete your body of fluid. Unlike mine, it needs water to function properly.'

A short while later, they came to a glade with a shimmering pool at its centre, and a cluster of Dingle Trees which bent over to shield them from the sun as they sat down on the soft grass. Zon dipped his finger into the pool, and pronounced it safe to drink; Brad drank his fill, and then replenished his carry bag with an assortment of fruit and nuts.

'How do you feel, now that we're back in the real world?' asked Brad, 'looking back, I feel it was all unreal somehow, down there.'

'It is good to be back in my world,' said Zon, 'and there are some things I must tell you, which I had not fully realised until we were on our way up. I was happy in my world, doing what I wanted, and free from fear, but things have changed since I found you. Before, I had not known the company we have now, and if it were to cease, I would feel lonely and sad.' he added, and then paused, 'I have learnt a lot from you. My way of looking at things and my way of thinking has changed. I am grateful for that.'

As their world swung around its sun, the Dingle Trees rustled as they reset their branches to shade the pair by the pool, and Brad felt a lump in his throat.

'I think it's time I said something too,' Brad responded at last, breaking the awkward silence, 'I have come to look upon you as another human being, strange as it may sound, and I enjoy your company very much. We make a good team with our different ways of thinking, and I can see no reason why this friendship should end. I too, would feel lonely if anything should happen to you. In fact, I think I would just give up.' and reached across to place his hand on Zon's. They sat there quietly in the warm air, drinking in the pleasant scene, and wondering if the underworld they had just visited was all a dream. Then Brad fell asleep, dreams of his own world coming and going, and Zon looked at the pictures in Brad's mind, adding to his vocabulary and understanding of his companion.

Eventually, the sun dipped below the horizon, the stars came out along with the usual meteor shower, and Zon was glad of the day he saw one which didn't burn up in the atmosphere. He would have shed a tear, if he had thought to include a tear duct to his eyes when he changed his body to match that of his friend.

Chapter 5
The final decision

'I HAVE COMPARED my world with this one,' said Brad, opening up the conversation, 'and I can see several differences which don't seem quite right. This world has no birds or reptiles, as far as I know. The insects are somewhat limited, as are the fish and animals. I would have expected many more varieties; nature always fills every nook and cranny, and here there are many gaps.' He paused to get his thoughts in order.

'I think this world only developed vegetation and was void of all animal life. It was visited by some alien race who, for whatever reason, decided to add animals, insects and fish in a limited numbers and variety - hence the underground complex and its assembly rooms. They must have tried many different types, hence the assortment we saw down below, only adding to the surface those few they thought most suited, and I think they tried them out in the caves down there, to see which were best.'

'What you say seems reasonable, bearing in mind what we have found,' said Zon, 'please carry on with your theory.'

'OK, this next idea may be a bit upsetting for you, but it's only my theory,' Brad said, 'I have no idea how they did it, but somehow, they were able to construct creatures from the bits and pieces they manufactured and add a life force to them. As far as I know, every living thing has a life force running it - some people call it a soul, a spirit, a unit of awareness. Call it what you will, it is the driving force of the creature. Insects probably have a lower level of awareness and intelligence, whereas human beings have one much higher - as far as I know. Some of my people consider themselves to be bodies - I don't, I think I am me, and I am in this body, running it. A lot of research has been done to prove that we exist as a separate entity - but not all believe it.'

'So far I agree with you,' said Zon, 'I have thought something along those lines about myself, but I do not have the certainty you have.'

'Are you sure you want me to carry on with this?' asked Brad, 'it is only my idea. You may have other thoughts on the matter.'

'Yes, please carry on,' Zon replied, 'at the moment I am not sure what to believe. I am feeling confused, and I do not like it.'

'Alright. I think they made your body, and gave it a life force - you.

God knows how they did it, or where you came from, but it is the only thing that makes any sense to me. From my point of view, I think you are the highest form I have ever come across. Nothing else I know of can change its shape to suit any circumstances as you can, it's a great ability. My hope is, as time goes on, we may be able to prove it, one way or the other, the life force thing - if you wish.'

The silence grew, and Brad thought it best to change the subject for a while.

'What I don't understand is why the aliens left their complex. Where did they go? There seems to be no trace of them, on the surface. If they had made this world more to their liking by adding the creatures they wanted, why are they not living in it? We still have a lot of unanswered questions; the thing is, do we go on trying to solve them, or just enjoy what we have here? What do you think?'

'At the moment, I would like to reflect on what we have found out, and enjoy our world,' replied Zon, 'I do not think we will ever solve all the mysteries.'

'I agree,' said Brad, 'it's all been a bit of an overwhelm. I think you're right; we should just take it easy for a while and let our thoughts settle down. Who knows, we may find out some more things as we wander around.'

They sat there by the pool in silence for a while, each thinking their own thoughts, and wondering what the other was thinking.

As the sun moved around, the two Dingle trees which had been shading them returned their branches back to their normal position, while the one on the other side bent several branches over, offering shade to the resting pair. Brad, meanwhile, had dozed off into a dream filled sleep, and Zon looked on unashamedly as the pictures in Brad's mind flashed by.

As the sun reached its zenith, the ground shook several times as another earth tremor rippled across Zon's world, relieving stresses which had built up, and Brad woke up with a start.

'What the h..... Oh, we've had another shaker,' he said to Zon, 'it's nothing to worry about,' he added, lying back on the soft grass, 'we often used to get them on my home world.' Zon made no comment, he had been pondering another problem.

'I have been thinking about the future,' said Zon, 'and the fact that your body is not like mine. From what I have learnt, your body will die one day, and I will be left without your company. It may seem selfish, but I do not like the idea, and I wondered if there might be a solution.'

'What do you have in mind?' asked Brad.

'If, when you are near death, I was to absorb your body, I may be able to absorb you as well. And we could share my body. It may seem a bit frightening to you, but please think about it. I do not want to be alone again.'

'Do you think it would work?' asked a startled Brad, 'I've never heard of such a thing before. How can two people share one body?'

'To be honest, I do not know. But I think it may be possible - it is just a feeling I have. Please give it some thought - I think you have plenty of time to do that.'

'But how would we talk to each other?' asked Brad, worried that he would be trapped in a body not his own, and unable to communicate.

'I can see your pictures when you think, and I can hear your words in those pictures. I think the whole thing may work in reverse, if we share the same space.'

'I'll certainly give it some thought,' said Brad, 'we may be able to set up some sort of experiment to prove it one way or the other. I would feel a lot happier about it then.'

Zon could feel the unease his friend was experiencing and decided to drop the subject for the time being - but it would not be forgotten.

'If you are rested enough, shall we continue down the valley?' asked Zon.

'Yep,' Brad replied, 'I can't help feeling there are more things the aliens have left behind to be discovered. It may give us a clue as to what they were really about.'

Shouldering his carry bag, Brad followed Zon down past the pool and into a narrow ravine, the sides of which were draped in what looked like fine strands of cotton. Thick patches of it hung from the protruding rocks, almost like fine cloth and gently swaying in the light breeze, while a sickly-sweet smell hung in the air.

'This reminds me of something,' said Brad, '....I know, spiders! Some of ours are poisonous, I hope these aren't. Hey, look at that,' he said, pointing, 'it looks as if something has been bundled up in that white stuff, and it's moving slightly.'

A small mound of fine white filaments was gently pulsating, as though something inside it was breathing slowly, and Zon went over to see what it was. A finger elongated, flattened, and slid into the white mass, followed by a soft tearing sound as Zon opened up the wrapping, exposing the body of an animal a little larger than a Rockcat, with a black and white striped coat.

'I have not seen this creature before,' said Zon, 'and it look as if something has put it to sleep, and then wrapped it up in these filaments. Perhaps it is the filament makers food store. Being asleep, it will not decompose as would normally happen.'

A sheet of the white stuff draped over a near by rock vibrated, and then swung aside to reveal a dark brown beetle-like creature about thirty centimetres long, and nearly as wide. Two pincer-like jaws clicked and rattled as the creature moved them to and fro, staring at them belligerently, and the pair stepped back in surprise. Zon quickly stepped forward again and peeled back the wrapping from the sleeping creature, scooping it up in his arms and ran for the end of the ravine.

'Quick Brad, run, we must leave this place!' Zon called out, 'I think that brown thing is not happy at what we have done.'

Brad did his best to follow Zon, but found he was staggering about instead of running in a straight line, and then he tripped and fell. A second later, and he felt a tug on his arm. Trying to fight it off for a moment, he realised that Zon had extended his arm and was dragging him free of the danger area.

'Thanks for that,' said a breathless Brad, scrambling to his feet, 'that was a close one. I just couldn't co-ordinate my legs - they felt like rubber. Did you notice that smell?'

'Yes, I think it is something like the flower you found in the caves, but it did not affect me. I wonder why?'

'As you say, you are different to me, so you would react differently, I suppose,' Brad replied, 'just as well in the circumstances.'

The creature they had rescued still lay in a dormant state on the grass, breathing slowly. One of Zon's fingers extruded a fine needle-like probe, and he inserted it into the unfortunate creature.

'I would think the brown thing wraps its food up to preserve it for later, but this is different. There are several small, pale-yellow balls inserted under the skin. I think this is its method of breeding more of the same. I will remove them, but I can not awaken the creature - perhaps if we put it somewhere safe, it will regain life.'

Zon carried the sleeping creature until they came to a high rock with a flat top, and extending his arm again, he placed it on top of the rock where it would be out of harms way. Brad was moved by the tenderness shown by Zon, and wondered if he had acquired some human traits during the period they had been together. Or was this a side of Zon he hadn't noticed before?

At the end of the valley, the ground levelled out to a flat plain of sand, with what looked like small pools of water dotted about, and Brad was looking forward to a cooling drink. Zon must have sensed his intentions.

'You will not find a drink out there,' he said, with a grin, 'it may look like water, but it is not.'

'How can you tell?' asked Brad, 'I can see it.' Zon just strode ahead.

As they came up to the first pool, it was evidentially not water, although from a distance it looked like it.

'What the hell is it?' asked Brad, annoyed at being fooled so easily, 'it looks solid.'

'I think it is something put there by the aliens,' Zon responded, 'it is certainly not something from nature.'

The round 'pools' seemed to be made of a glass-like substance, with flecks of some metallic material embedded within - and then they noticed the regular pattern they formed.

'It doesn't look as if it does anything,' said Brad, stamping on one to see how solid it really was, 'but it must have a purpose. Maybe it's a form of communicator to an orbiting mother ship - or even another world. Do you think we should destroy it in case it sends messages of what we've been up to?'

'I do not think we need worry about it,' Zon replied, 'remember, the complex had been abandoned a long time ago. Why they went away I do not know, but I doubt they have any interest in it now.'

Brad managed to get his fingers under the edge of the 'pool' and tried to lift it up, but it was firmly locked into the surrounding sand.

'Are you greatly in need of water?' asked Zon, 'We could go back if need be.'

'No, I have plenty of fruit in my bag, and some of it is mainly water, much like something we call a melon - it's almost as good as a drink.'

The pair set off on the long journey across the sand plain, Brad wondering if he had been wise about not returning to fill up with water - it was too late now, they were committed.

Part way across, Zon saw something moving; it looked like a piece of rope, wriggling about like a very long snake. As they got closer, they could see it was along procession of small animals, about fifteen centimetres long, nose to tail, heading across the direction they were travelling in.

'What the hell are those?' exclaimed Brad, 'surely they'll never make it across the plain at that speed.'

'It is similar to a creature I have seen before, but they usually go around in pairs,' said Zon, 'let us go to the head of the line to see what is driving them.'

It didn't take long for them to stride out and reach the head of the column, but the one in the lead was twice the size of the others, and looked different somehow. Using his foot, Zon turned the lead creature to one side, but it hissed at him, and turned back to its original path.

'I think they know where they are going. At least the one leading them does, I would assume they have done this journey before.' Zon did something with his eyes, and then in a surprised voice announced that the line of creatures stretched back nearly as far as they had travelled themselves.

Leaving the train of nose to tail creatures to their own devices, the pair set off for the distant band of green which heralded some respite from the blazing sun, and where shade, food, and water could be obtained. Brad was getting parched.

The sun had begun it's journey down to the horizon by the time they had reached the tree line, and the first request from Brad was for a drink. Zon quickly located a small stream, and Brad indulged in a long drink and then stripped to the skin for a rather shallow bath, much to the amusement of Zon, who somehow didn't need to bathe.

'How come you have no body odour?' asked Brad, scrubbing hard those parts of his body which were most offensive to him, 'I thought all creatures sweated. It's a means of getting rid of toxins and excess salts. Also, it regulates the body's temperature.'

'I have never thought about it,' Zon replied, 'my temperature always remains the same, as far as I know. But I do not find your body smell unpleasant. I think if you did not wash at all, your body would stabilise, and there would be no smell.'

With the food bag replenished and Brad having eaten his fill, the pair settled down for a good night's rest. Well, Brad did, Zon remained alert throughout the hours of darkness.

Next morning, Brad noticed that Zon seemed preoccupied with something, and asked what it was.

'I have been thinking,' he said, 'looking at the pictures which run through your mind, you would need a female partner to make your life more complete. Nearly all of the people you know on your home world seem to. Even some of the creatures on my world pair up for life, so there must be something beneficial in doing so.'

'Yes, I agree with that,' Brad replied, briefly remembering the joys of female companionship, 'but I do not have any option here. There's just you and me, and I don't think we can send for a mail-order blond,' he added with a chuckle.

'That is the point I am raising,' Zon replied, 'remember, I can adopt any shape I care to, and it would be quite possible to duplicate your female form, and all which that implies, if you so wish.'

For a brief moment Brad was tempted, and then a feeling of revulsion swept through him, and he shuddered.

'It's very kind of you,' Brad said, 'but I don't think you quite understand. It would not be the same as a real human woman. There's more to it than what you've seen in my mind - it's hard to explain. I appreciate your offer, but I think we had better leave things as they are. I find your companionship most agreeable, and we make a good team.'

'If that is your wish,' said Zon, 'I was just looking at the practicalities of a human's needs. As you say, there is something I do not understand - but I will try to.'

Feeling a bit embarrassed and hoping he had not offended Zon in any way, Brad rearranged the food in his carry bag as something to do to cover an awkward moment. And then they were off again, threading their way through the cool green shade of the ever-thickening forest, the trees growing taller and their trunks thicker as they progressed.

They stopped at the foot of one enormous specimen, gazing up into the tangle of branches as they reached high up into the sky.

'I have never seen a tree as tall as that,' said Brad, and we have some really big ones. How about climbing it?'

'I can, but you will have a problem in getting up the first part - there are no branches for you to climb. If you wish, I will go up first, and then I can haul you up to the first branches. From then on you will be able to climb yourself, but be careful. If you fall, I will lose my friend.' Brad nodded.

Zon reached up to the massive trunk, extended what looked like a fearsome set of claws, and proceeded to shin up the rough bark at a speed which left Brad opened mouthed. A long rope like arm dropped down next to Brad, twisted around his waist, and he was airborne.

'Please be careful,' said Zon,' there maybe some odd creatures up here which may frighten you for a moment, so do not lose your grip.'

It took a long time for the pair to reach the highest branches, with many a stop on the way, but the view from the top was well worth it, according to Brad. Zon made little comment, apart from the time it had taken.

'What's that?' said Brad, pointing to a shiny object about five kilometres away in a clearing, 'it looks like something metal - unless it's water.'

Zon elongated his eyes, as he did to view long distant objects.

'I think it is the vehicle those unpleasant people came in, the ones I had to send into the sinking sands. Do you wish to go and see it?'

'You bet I do,' replied Brad, hardly able to conceal his excitement, 'the chance to see an alien space craft is one thing I don't want to pass up.' and Brad began the long scramble down the mighty tree.

'Be careful,' called out Zon, 'we have all the time we need. It will still be there tomorrow.'

By the time they had reached the ground, it was getting dark, and they rested for the night after a meal, and a long discussion about the possibility of aliens on other worlds. As soon as the sun broke the horizon, they headed off to find the alien craft, Brad asking how Zon knew where it lay, as the forest all looked the same.

'I just know, somehow. I always know where I am,' he said, which didn't answer the question, as far as Brad was concerned.

When they came to the clearing in the forest, the alien craft was much bigger than the one Brad had arrived in, and somehow looked ugly - with bits and pieces sticking out from the main body. Brad wondered how the appendages had survived the heat of entry into the atmosphere at high speed. He would have expected them to burn up, but then he thought being alien, it may have had a different method of entry - he would find out.

On close inspection, the craft did look a bit battered, and the aliens had not bothered to close the hatchway properly when leaving it.

'Safe enough to go in?' Brad enquired.

'I would think so,' Zon replied, 'there is nothing alive in there after all this time. But do not twiddle with anything, it may still have a means of flying.'

Brad couldn't open the hatch, the hinges had corroded over the years, and it took Zon's mighty strength to force the reluctant hatch to give way - and then they were in.

Inside there were two rows of crude seats, a rack containing what they thought were weapons of some sort, and a series of cupboards along one wall. Up forward was a small compartment with one seat where the pilot must have sat, and an array of control switches and knobs which made little sense to either of them.

'If we could power this thing up, we could travel around your world at great speed,' said Brad, enthusiastically, 'and see a lot more - even over the great sea you mentioned.'

'It is a possibility,' Zon replied, 'but not one I would recommend. You may be able to make this thing rise into the air, but press the wrong control, and it could plummet down. I may survive the crash, but I doubt your body would. I am sorry, but I will have no part of it.'

Brad was surprised at Zon's firm insistence, but saw the sense in it - reluctantly.

They left the alien craft to continue to degrade in blazing sun, after all, it didn't really belong there.

Over the years, they visited the caverns again and again, exploring ever deeper to marvel at the odd creations the aliens had experimented with, discarding most as unfit for the surface; but they continued to multiply in the caves, some cross breeding and bringing forth even more bizarre creations.

One day they came to a huge river, slow and wide. Brad suggested they construct a raft from fallen trees and float down it to see what was at the end - and so they did. After many days, they came to the mouth of the river where it joined the great sea, and were amazed at the massive waves which came crashing ashore, sending clouds of spray high into the air.

'I wonder what creatures we'll find in there,' Brad said.

'I don't think we could get our raft past those huge waves - it would break up,' said Zon, 'although I am as curious as you - I think we will have to bypass this one.'

Brad's skin was darkening due to the bright sunlight, and he now had a deep tan, complete with a set of wrinkles a mole rat would have been proud of. His joints didn't work quite as well, and Zon had to keep repairing them so that they could keep travelling.

One day, they were climbing a particularly difficult group of rocks, as there seemed to be a something flashing somewhere near the top and Brad insisted they find out what it was. He slipped and went crashing to the ground. Zon slithered down as fast as he could to try and get there first to cushion Brad's fall, but failed. Brad's crumpled body lay still, with his limbs bent in awkward directions, and Zon knew his friend's life was possibly near its end - there was just too much damage to rebuild - even for him. He straightened out Brad's body as best as he could, and then one eye opened.

'Sorry, I slipped,' Brad managed to get out, 'can you do anything to ease the pain? I'm all busted up, and it hurts like hell.' Zon, for the first time, felt panic.

'I think the time has come for a decision to be made. I do not think I can repair your body. It is too badly damaged, with many bones broken, and there is blood coming from a head wound and several other places. Do you remember we once talked of becoming one? The time has come to decide if you would be willing to try it. I think it will work, and there are no other options open to us.'

'OK, how will you do it?' Brad's voice was getting fainter.

'I will encase your body with mine and reach out to you. It may feel strange, but be willing to join me. If we can become one, we can still enjoy each other's company - we still have a lot of exploring to do.'

'Please do something, I can't stand this pain much longer,' Brad just about managed to get out, before his vision dimmed.

Zon stretched himself out flat, extended two arms and rolled the now still and crumpled body of Brad into the middle of his flattened form. Slowly the edges curled up and over Brad until there was just one amorphous lump on the ground, and then it slowly changed shape to become humanoid again.

'I can feel you here,' Zon said, 'reach out to me.'

'Good God, I can see,' exclaimed a startled Brad, 'and more clearly than before. You've done it - I am alive, and the pain has gone. Where are you?'

'I am here, besides you. We are one now. We share all our thoughts and feelings - I am so glad.'

'Where is my body?' asked Brad, still a little confused, 'there is only one person standing here - and that's me, but it's your body.'

'I absorbed your body, keeping some parts for now - the rest is on the ground behind us.'

Brad turned his head, and there on the ground was a slushy mess, slowly sinking into the porous sand.

'It will take a little while for you to get used to sharing with me,' said Zon, 'but it will become more natural with time - and we have plenty of that. Sometimes I will have to take over from you if circumstances need a very quick response, but apart from that, I will leave you in control of our movements.'

'I can hardly believe this' said Brad, still trying to come to terms with the seemingly impossible, 'it feels like my body, but... God, this is bloody fantastic... I'mlost for words.'

'If it makes you feel more comfortable, I can make two mouthpieces, so that we can talk vocally. But it is not really necessary.'

'No, it's fine, I can hear you clearly. It must be some form of telepathy, I suppose,' said Brad, 'as you say, this is going to take a bit of getting used to.'

The body containing the beings of Zon and Brad walked over to a rock, and sat down. Brad felt as he had in his old body, but without the pains and creaky knees. His vision had improved, as had many other senses, and he felt young again - no, ageless.

The exploration of the planet continued for the pair, and many more wondrous things were found - but not all understood by them.

A very long time ago, the aliens in the deep caves had created many strange and wonderful creatures, most of which still resided in the caves. But none were stranger than Zon's body, with its impossible morphing abilities. And then there was Zon himself - where did he come from?

Inadvertently, the aliens had brought about a unique mixture of humanoid and a new creature, combining Brad's logical approach and scientific knowledge with Zon's compassion, deep understanding of life forms and those things which really mattered.

The aliens attempt at creating humanoids was not to their satisfaction, after those in the 'monastery' developed strange and cruel habits, observed by another attempt, the 'watchers' - and when they failed it had been decided to erase the whole setup. Why the aliens left was also a puzzle, as was their reason for populating this world with new life in the first place.

One day, they were sitting on top of Zon's favourite mountain top looking out over the rolling hills and valleys to the barren lands where Brad's escape module had crashed, and recalling the moment when Zon had found his companion.

'I have had an idea,' said Zon, after a long pause, 'as far as I know, we shall live forever. I have outlived all the creatures I have ever found here, many times over, and a thought struck me… What if we could divide somehow, become two, then more?'

THE END
If you have enjoyed this book, please consider leaving a review on Amazon. It would mean a lot to us.

About the Author

"Back in 1998 I was commenting to a friend that I didn't go much on so called modern Science Fiction. It didn't seem as good or as interesting as the adventures stories written by the old masters of sci-fi – Clarke, Russell, Pohl, Asimov, Heinlein etc. His reaction was 'well, write your own then' – As I already had an idea at the back of my mind, I did. After printing up ten copies and binding them (hardback) they were passed around among like minded friends – and then came the request for more of the same! Again and again. Only one problem – I was spending too much time printing and binding and not writing, which I enjoy. Getting into 'print' is difficult – if not impossible – so I chose the 'eBook' route. I would recommend it to anyone who likes writing, and has a story to tell."

David (aka D.B) Reynolds-Moreton is a retired research and development engineer who lives in Devon, England with his wife. You can read a short biography of his life and adventures in science at :

www.sci-fi-cafe.com/david-reynolds-moreton